DILEMMAS

by
CRYSTAL KINN-TARVER

DILEMMAS
by
CRYSTAL KINN-TARVER

© 2020 by Crystal Kinn-Tarver
All rights reserved.

This book and no parts thereof may be reproduced, stored in a retrieval system, or transmitted in any form by any means—electronic, mechanical, photocopy, recording, or otherwise—without written permission from the publisher.

This is a work of fiction. Any resemblance to actual events, locales, or persons, living or dead, is entirely coincidental.

Cover Designed by: Dynasty's Visionary Designs

Edited by: Gloria Palmer
movinonup57@yahoo.com

Published by: Casey Carter
Authorcaseycarter@gmail.com

ISBN-13: 9-7987-2183835-4

Acknowledgements/Dedication

I would like to thank the Highest Almighty Power above, my God, for blessing me with the gift of storytelling. He made me the creative, imaginative creature I am today. Thank you to my husband, Joe, for encouraging me to be a better me. You have stood by me through the thick, thin, bad, and ugly. Thanks for loving me unconditionally. Thank you for three children—Dennis, Joseph, and Jolante—for being the reason I grind and hustle like I do. You all have taught me so much. We literally grew up with each other. I've always wanted to show you there's a better way. Work harder now so you can work smarter later.

To my mother, Pauline: I miss you so much. What's understood doesn't need to be explained. Thank you, Daddy, for teaching me how to cook! Because of you, all your kids can burn in the kitchen! You also taught me how to hit the highway! Rule number one: You only stop when it's time to get gas, so you'd better not drink too much! Lol! Thank you to my godfather/grandfather/stepfather, Larry Taylor. I wouldn't be the person I am, if you hadn't come into my life. It amazes me that you were able to treat someone else's children like your own. Making you Dennis' godfather was one of the best decisions I ever made. Thank you for being a consistent role model in my life.

To my siblings, Tracy, Lionel, Terrence, Gabe, Bianca, Tyesha, and Camarie: I love you all immensely. I love the fact that Daddy made sure we all knew each other. We are a strong, opinionated bunch. Hopefully, we can get a sibling trip popping soon. I can't forget my deceased siblings, Lamont Jr., Andrea, and finally, Ebony Kinn. Little Sista, I miss you more than you will ever know. Although we were like oil and water, I would do anything to protect you. I hate that you had to die at the hands of a cowardly-ass mofo. Rest in heaven.

To my Standberry/Kinn family: Thank you for the get togethers, family trips, cook out, and celebrations. It's always a party when we link up. The Standberry's will turn a party inside out and upside down! Lol.

To my extended family, my in laws, The Tarvers, Smiths, and Hales: Y'all are more like my blood family instead of my in-laws. We've been rocking together for almost thirty years! Every birthday, celebration, and holiday, we have partied! An awesome example of a close-knit family. Theresa Smith, my second mother, my mother-in-law: I will never forget you. Rest in heaven.

To my friends, my DAY ONES!, Rose, Shanavia, December, Tracy H., and Dana Dane: Thank you for the encouraging, motivating, and supporting words. Thanks for being there every step of the way. My sister/cousin, Talika: Thank you for being my rock. You became my sister after losing my sister. I can't thank you enough for your support and for being level-headed.

Cover Girls Book Club!!!!! A bunch of beautiful women who are so diversified. I have learned so much from every one of you. Thank you for all being my first critics. Love y'all!

"Protection is an everlasting necessity that leaves one hell of an impression. The only thing that will keep me from wanting or having it is death."
~ Anonymous

Table of Contents

Acknowledgements/Dedication	iii
Prologue	1
Rakeem	1
Eight Years Earlier	7
~ One ~	9
Rakeem	9
~ Two ~	17
Sheree	17
~ Three ~	27
Sheree	27
~ Four ~	31
Rakeem	31
~ Five ~	46
Sheree	46
~ Six ~	54
Rakeem	54
~ Seven ~	75
Sheree	75
The Present	85
~ Eight ~	87
Courtney	87

~ Nine ~	90
Rakeem	90
~ Ten ~	96
Sheree	96
~ Eleven ~	100
Courtney	100
~ Twelve ~	105
Rakeem	105
~ Thirteen ~	122
Courtney	122
~ Fourteen ~	124
Rakeem	124
~ Fifteen ~	129
Sheree	129
~ Sixteen ~	135
Courtney	135
~ Seventeen ~	142
Rakeem	142
~ Eighteen ~	146
Courtney	146
~ Nineteen ~	151
Sheree	151
~ Twenty ~	156
Rakeem	156
~ Twenty-One ~	161
Courtney	161

~ Twenty-Two ~	174
Sheree	174
~ Twenty-Three ~	183
Rakeem	183
~ Twenty-Four ~	193
Courtney	193
~ Twenty-Five ~	202
Alexis	202
~ Twenty-Six ~	209
Courtney	209
~ Questions ~	215
Coming Soon	217
The Dom	217
Prologue	217

DILEMMAS

Prologue

Rakeem

'Here I am, fifty years old, and for the third time, standing at the altar, waiting on my bride-to-be.'

Like the other times, I am questioning my decision. I really care for Courtney. No! I love Courtney! See what I mean? This shit is not cool! I shouldn't have these types of doubts! I should be nervous! Crying! Excited! But I'm not! I want to marry Courtney and get this day over with so she can stop nagging the shit out of me about this marriage thing. If it were left to me, I would have just shacked up with her without a formal engagement.

Courtney is fifty-two years old, no kids, and has never been married. We have only been in a relationship for eight months, and truthfully, I can't tell you how we got here. I just remember her pressuring me about changing my Facebook status from "single" to "relationship". I guess in her eyes that solidified our "relationship". Truthfully, I didn't care because I didn't have anything going on.

The only person I am remotely close to being involved with is involved with someone else. Clearly, there is no end in sight for them, which means there is no beginning for us, but one can hope, right? Man, I do love her though. I will always love her, but I can't wait on her forever and I refuse to grow old alone. So, if marrying Courtney is what I have to do to keep her happy and in my life, I will make that sacrifice once again.

I am brought out of my trance by the sound of music. The ceremony is about to start.

'Fuck! I guess there ain't no getting out of this shit. Maybe I should fake sick or faint! Hell yeah! If I faint right here, I can get out of this shit and prolong the wedding for another year."

I should be the ma'fucka walking down the aisle, considering Courtney proposed to me! Right in front of all my friends and family! How could I say no? She'd looked so…. desperate! If I had said no, I wouldn't be standing at the altar, y'all would be crying over my casket! Did I forget to mention that Courtney has a few screws loose? But that's another story for another day.

The instrumental versions of all my favorite songs begin to play. Ed Sheeran's song, *Thinking Out Loud*, comes on.

> *And I'm thinking 'bout how people fall in love in love in mysterious ways*
> *Maybe just the touch of a hand*
> *Oh, me, I fall in love with you every single day*
> *And I just wanna tell you I am….*
> *Oh, maybe we found love right here we are*
> *And we found love right where we are…*

'Damn, that's OUR song,' I think, shaking my head. No matter what I do or who I'm with, I can never get HER out of my head or heart. *'Why didn't I make a new playlist?'*

I can't tell you when the doors of the church opened or when the wedding started because I am thinking about HER. By the time I tune back in, my groomsmen are alongside me and the bridesmaids are on the opposite side. The preacher tells everyone to rise as my wife-to-be is about to make an entrance. As the double doors open, I see Courtney standing there, looking beautiful as usual, but something else catches my eye—or should I say, someone. Is that... Nope, I am seeing things; she wouldn't dare!

Courtney proceeds down the aisle, showing all thirty-two teeth. I have to put on a fake smile and pretend to be remotely interested, when in the back of my mind I'm waiting for those damn doors to open again to confirm my suspicion. Courtney is now standing in front of me at the altar with her old-ass, sanctified daddy.

"Who gives this lady to this man?" says Pastor Jackson.

"I do," I hear Mr. Benson say.

Suddenly, I hear the squeaking of doors. My eyes dart in that direction. Late arrivals are entering the church and taking their places on the groom's or the bride's side. Courtney's side is more packed than mine. I didn't invite a lot of people, figuring this was marriage number three, so why bother. It is like a female who keeps having babies and wanting a baby shower for each kid. Eventually, people are gonna say, "Hell, I'm not about to keep going to these showers only for her to have another baby next year." It goes the same for weddings.

Then... I see HER! It's really HER! How the fuck did she find out I'm getting married? Let alone when and where the wedding is!

That damn Courtney! That woman posts everything for the Book or the Gram. Seriously! We can't even go to the mall without her making a post about it. If anyone was ever looking to kill me, just check Facebook or Instagram and I'm as good as dead!

Sheree is the last person to walk—more like glide—through the door, wearing a white form-fitting maxi-dress that hugs all her curves. She has a large white flower on the left side of her head behind her ear. She looks as if she is walking directly toward me. I am paralyzed; I can't move. She is now ten aisles away from me. What the fuck is she doing? Then she stops. I can hear whispering from people in the congregation, mainly from my side of the room because everyone who knows me knows Sheree. I don't realize I'm squeezing Courtney's hands so hard until she pinches me. That breaks Sheree's and my stare. Courtney looks over her shoulder to see why I am so distracted, then glares back at me as to say, "I don't give a fuck who that is, you'd better not embarrass me."

Sheree takes a seat near one of my friends where she can continue to interrogate me with those honey-brown eyes. Pastor Jackson starts talking some mumble-jumble about the bond not being broken and the wedding band is a circle. Blah blah blah…

"Do you, Rakeem Stafford, take Courtney Monique Benson to be your lawfully-wedded wife?"

I can feel Sheree's eyes burning a hole in the side of my head, and I can see the fire coming from the top of Courtney's veil. If looks could kill…

I guess I've hesitated too long for her liking because I feel another pinch. This time, I shoot her a look that says, "If you do that shit again, I'ma give ya ass something to cry about." She gets the hint.

"I do," I manage to say.

"Courtney Monique Benson, do you take Rakeem Stafford to be your lawfully wedded hus—"

"I do," she says before the pastor can get the words out his mouth.

Everybody laughs. Not me. I don't see shit funny. She's acting thirsty… dehydrated.

"If there's anyone here who feels this man and this woman should not be married, speak now or forever hold your peace…"

I think I stop breathing when I see Sheree stand up. Everyone gasps and looks at Sheree. She walks toward the aisle and looks at Courtney and me. She opens her mouth to speak—just as Courtney faints in my arms.

EIGHT YEARS EARLIER

~ One ~

Rakeem

Chilling in the city was starting to get old. I was use to not looking over my shoulder or carrying my piece, but sometimes I had to get out the house. Baby-momma and kids were cool, but I needed a break. I decided to head to the city to catch up with my niggas I knew from the hood. We go way back to middle school days. I didn't hang with them often, but they were still my niggas for life. No one fucked with me. Although I was only five-eight, I had the heart, swag, and confidence of a nigga six feet tall.

"Man, how is family life for you in the suburbs?" said Scoot.

"It's all good, my nigga, just working and raising these kids."

"I hear that shit. I'm tryna do the same. My girl's pregnant again."

"Damn, nigga, how many does that make now?"

"Number eight, but you can't talk Keem. Shit, you only three shy from me."

"Yeah, nigga, *behind* you. I'm thinking about getting clipped. I don't want anymore. Fuck that!"

"Whatever, nigga. Ain't no one touching my shit."

"Obviously someone's touching yo' shit." I laughed.

There was a knock on the door. Scoot's girl Lolo went to answer it. In walked a nice, slim chick with big breasts and a small frame. She wasn't the cutest, but she was sexy as fuck! She had on this cute pink-and-white dress that resembled something you would see Serena or Venus playing tennis in. Her calves were nice and strong, like she ran marathons. Her hair was in a cute wrap that hung close to her shoulders. Her skin was the color of honey and she had the fullest set of lips. They looked so soft, even without gloss on them. Man, I wish I could kiss them.

"Who is ol' girl, Scoot?" I asked.

"That was the homie, Chuck's, girl, but they ain't together no more."

"Oh, that nigga's out?"

"Yeah."

"Well, introduce me, dog."

"Man, I told you she's Chuck's ex."

"Didn't you say ex?"

Scoot nodded his head.

"Okay, introduce us; that's yo nigga, not mine. I don't owe him shit."

"Yeah, but you know how that nigga is."

Scoot was referring to Chuck's hot-headed shenanigans and demeanor, but I didn't give a fuck about that shit. I would lay that nigga down if I had to.

"Man, I don't give a fuck about how that nigga is."

I was getting heated because this nigga was acting scared as fuck of this nigga and he wasn't even in our presence. Scoot still didn't budge, so I took matters in my own hands.

"What's up, Lolo? Introduce me to your homegirl."

"Keem, this is my girl, Sheree, Sheree, this is Scoot's boy, Keem." Lolo chuckled.

Sheree extended her hand, looked me directly in my eyes, and said, "How are you doing, Keem? Nice to meet you."

"Nice to meet you as well, Sweetie. Nice dress."

"Thanks for the compliment, babe."

After she called me babe, I prayed she would never call me by my real name again. I wanted to be 'babe' forever to her. Damn, I was bugging! I had only met this girl for five minutes, and she had me wanting to change my name to 'babe. Chuck done fucked up because ol' girl was gonna be mine. I didn't give a fuck if it was only for one night.

We must have talked that nigga Chuck up because he came waltzing through the door like he was the man. I laid back in the cut and observed how the other niggas swung from his balls. He and Sheree made small talk before they walked out the door together. I tried to ear hustle but couldn't make out anything until I heard Sheree yell at him to let her arm go. That was my cue to interrupt their conversation and put that nigga in his place. Then he got the hell on and we enjoyed the rest of the night.

Shorty and I made small talk as Scoot and a couple of niggas from the hood played dominos. I learned she worked as a customer service rep at a small but reputable company in Royal Oak. She had two teenage kids, one boy and one girl. She loved music, poetry, and wine. She was so laid back—until she got buzzed. Once she was buzzed, she was loud and hood as fuck. But I didn't mind at all; it was kind of sexy.

She had a New York accent although she'd grown up on the eastside of Detroit. I purposely didn't ask her if she had a boyfriend because I didn't want her to say yes. Nor did I want her to ask me if I had a woman. I didn't want to ruin what we had before it started.

Hours passed and it was getting late. I knew if I didn't get home, my girl would be blowing up my phone, which would lead to an argument, which would lead to a long, miserable weekend.

We exchanged numbers with hopes of hooking up later.

As I was driving home, my phone started to ring. I knew it was my girl by the ring tone I had assigned to her.

"Where are you?" questioned Brittany.

"On my way home; what's up?" I was getting annoyed with her checking me.

"It's two in the morning."

"I know the time; I'm looking at it."

"Don't get smart."

"Then don't be questioning me. I'll be there in a minute." I hung up before she could start talking shit.

My phone rang again, but it wasn't Brittany this time. It was Sheree.

"Hello."

"Hey, stranger; how's your drive?"

"It's cool, smooth sailing this time of the morning. How far is your drive?"

"About ten minutes or so, but I can talk to you until you make it home... if you want."

"That's cool," I said, trying not to sound too excited. "So, when can I see you again?"

I hadn't made it home, yet I was already making plans to see her again. This was not good.

"That would be up to you. I hear you're shacked up with a whole gang of kids." She laughed.

I didn't find that shit funny at all. I was going to have to have a little one-on-one talk with Lolo. She ain't had no business telling my business before I had a chance to tell my business.

"Oh yeah? Who'd you hear that from? Lolo?"

"You know I did. Come on now. I had to get the scoop on you. She didn't volunteer the information; I asked her for it."

"Oh, so you were checking on a brother, huh? You could have asked me, you know?

"I know, but I didn't want you to water down your situation by telling me you and her 'aren't like that' or 'you're just there for the kids'. Blah, blah blah."

"I got you. So, what about you?"

"What about me?"

This girl has a smart-ass mouth,' I thought, shaking my head.

"Do you have a man?"

"Not now. I was in a long-term relationship that ended about six months ago. Then I met Chuck, but that didn't work out, so I'm back single again—for now. By the way, thank you for what you did for me. I don't know what would have happened if you hadn't intervened."

"No need to thank me. I did what any real man would do if he saw a woman being assaulted."

"Yeah, I guess."

When I didn't respond, she proceeded.

"My ex and I have discussed reconciling, but not sure if that's going to happen."

"Yeah, I know how that goes," I said, thinking of my own situation. "So, back to my original question, when can I see you again?"

"Aww, are you missing me already, Keemie?" She laughed.

"Nah, I'm just trying to get to know you a little better, that's all."

"Yeah, okay. Let me find out you're catching feelings for ya girl this early in the game... You know us Leo's are quite addictive." She laughed again.

She ain't never lied. I hadn't had too many run-ins with Leo's. I was a Taurus, and a true Taurus too! Stubborn as fuck and set in my ways. Tyrese's song rang in my head. The part where he sings, *"I don't know what it is, but those Leo's drive me crazy."* Yeah, that part. I was in deep thought, wondering what the hell that nigga meant by that. I wish I could ask his ass. Damn!

"Keem! Keem!"

I could hear the panic in her voice. "Yeah, my bad. I'm here."

"I thought you had fallen asleep at the wheel. You scared me."

"Don't let me find out you care about a brotha already." I laughed, mocking her earlier comment. "You were about to start crying, huh? Keem! Keem!" I mocked her again.

"Oh, that's funny to you, huh? I just saved your life! You know you were sleep—or daydreaming about me. Now which one was it?"

I was shocked. I couldn't say anything. She'd straight up read my ass!

"Yeah, like I thought—you were daydreaming about me. Don't let me find out—"

"Whatever," I cut her off. "I was paying attention to the road. No daydreaming here, sweetie."

"Uh huh, sure you weren't."

And she was cocky as hell. Smh...

"I'm home now. Thanks for keeping me company on my way home," I said, not wanting to really end our conversation. "And you never answered my question."

"Okay, and to answer your question, soon. Real soon. Good night, Keemie, and don't dream about me too much." She chuckled.

"Good night, sweetie. I'll try not to."

I hung up the phone knowing damn-well she was going to be all in my thoughts and dreams tonight. This was not looking good. I was already fiending for her and she didn't even know it.

~ Two ~

Sheree

Last night was awesome. I hadn't felt this way about a dude in a long time. Although I would never admit it to him, it felt like love at first sight. In just a short few hours, I felt as if I'd found HIM! I was not that chick who fell head over heels when first meeting a dude. I'd kissed plenty of frogs. Most were nothing more than for sex and/or company. I enjoyed their company until I got bored, then I move on—until I met Menard.

He was a cool guy who wouldn't take no for an answer. He'd had to grow on me. I think I was attracted to him because he was the opposite of me. I was loud and outspoken, and he was quiet and laid back. Everything was good for several years, but I felt we were growing apart. He worked afternoons and I worked mornings; plus, I went to school. We became two ships passing in the night. We broke up, went our separate ways, and hooked up from time to time, but the sparks were no longer there.

Meeting Keem was like a breath of fresh air. Yeah, he had a girlfriend, but that wasn't my problem. Besides at that point, we weren't doing anything wrong, just getting to know each other. Who knows, he might not be the one and this might be just be a fling. I kept telling myself I had no expectations so I wouldn't be disappointed if things didn't work out.

I was a firm believer that you don't meet the actual person until six-to-nine months into knowing them. The person you meet in the beginning is the person they believe *you* want *them* to be, but slowly and surely, the "real" them comes out. Think I'm joking? The more time you spend with a person, the more you start to see little things about them: shavings in the sink, drinking habits seem to increase, or they go from only smoking one blunt a day to smoking ounces. Hell! I dated a guy who'd managed to hide that he smoked cigarettes for a whole damn year! He nor his house ever smelled like cigarettes, so I was clueless that he was addicted to the white girl with the blonde hair.

Anyway, once the dust settled after the "probationary period" and both parties felt the same about each other, the relationship had a fighting chance. The probationary period was always a problem for me. I have a strong personality, and it can be overwhelming and intimidating to some. Everyone is not for everyone. So, if you are easily scared off by a female with a "ness" on the end—sassiness, cockiness, and aggressiveness—then I'm not the woman for you. I try to keep it up front and honest to avoid the bullshit and weed out the peons, but sometimes, it's unavoidable.

Growing up, I was never thought to be the pretty girl. In middle school, I was a skinny little girl with big breasts. My whole family had jheri curls because it was easy for my mom to manage. I use to dream of the day the curl in the back would touch the bottom of my neck. If you had long jheri curls, you were the shit! I never achieved "hang-time" status. When the phase was over, I went back to trying to manage my hair on my own. Epic fail.

As a grown woman, I still didn't consider myself cute or pretty, but that didn't bother me none. I was sexy! That was more satisfying to me than being pretty or cute.

Pretty and cute were for babies, puppies, or kittens. Men dated pretty and cute girls, but they usually didn't keep them, and if they kept them, it never stopped them from cheating on them. They wanted a woman with sex appeal.

Men found my full lips very attractive—unfortunately, for obvious reasons. They always wanted to kiss them or fantasize about how they would feel wrapped around their manhood. My size thirty-eight double D's were a little too much for my one hundred forty pound, five-four frame. I wore my hair in a wrap that finally touched the mole located right above my breasts. My smooth cinnamon skin was a mixture of my mulatto father and dark chocolate mother. It had a red tint to it that was somewhat exotic in the summer after lying out in the sun. During the winter months, I was easily several shades lighter. I wasn't curvaceous, but you couldn't tell I didn't have a whole lot of hips and ass the way I swung them from side-to-side. I commanded and demanded attention when I walked in a room. Even if it was only for a moment, give me my time, then you could go back to your regularly-scheduled program.

I wasn't expecting to meet anyone the day I met Keem. I'd worn a simple dress that clung to my flat stomach and gave my booty a little pop. I'd left the top two buttons unfastened to show a little cleavage. There were lots of guys in and out of Scoot and Lolo's house, but they weren't worth my time. No fresh haircuts or crispy new gym shoes were in the house. An instant turn-off... until I saw Keem.

I did a quick glance over before turning my head. Air Force Ones were crispy and white, just like his white tee.

Brand-new dark blue denim Levi's, and a freshly-shaved bald head. On his hip appeared to be a black, nine-millimeter Glock, secured in the holster. He had the prettiest set of teeth and he was bow-legged as shit! He wasn't the tallest in the room, but his presence and the respect everyone showed him made him appear taller than his five-eight height.

And his cologne... my gawd, this nigga smelled good. I had never smelled Creed until I smelled it on this man, and it smelled so delicious! That scent on that day would always be embedded in my nostrils. I low-key watched him as he worked the room. He had a red cup in his hand, reminiscing about the old days. They were deep in conversation when Chuck walked in the house.

All the niggas flocked to Chuck like he was a star or something. All of them except Keem. He stayed in the background and waited for all the niggas to stop swinging from Chuck's nuts. Me, I continued to stay seated and unphased. I hadn't talked to Chuck since our breakup. He had done and said some foul shit to me. That, along with the fact that he was a grimy-ass nigga, didn't sit well with me.

Chuck was a handsome-ass guy, sexy as hell in fact. When I heard he had been recently released from prison for aggravated assault and attempted robbery, I was reluctant to get involved with him, but he'd served his time and paid his debt to society. He was a smooth talker, easy on the eyes, and had that thug mentality a lot of us females from the hood can appreciate. He stood about six-four, with beautiful brown skin, beautiful teeth, and was very intimidating to those around him.

I think that was what attracted me to him. Like me, his presence intimidated people, but in different ways. People were intimidated by my demeanor, my presence, and my confidence. Chuck was a big, cocky dude (thanks to lifting weights in prison), so people were intimidated by his size, his voice, and his actions. He kept a gang of flunkies around who feared him. He was the Suge Knight of his click and had no problem making examples out of people if they tested his gangster.

I witnessed an incident when one of his little flunkies got mouthy and decided to question his authority regarding a "lick" they were going to hit later in the week. Chuck picked him up off the floor by his neck with one hand and scared the piss out of him—literally! He told him, the next time he opened his mouth to question his authority, he would cut his tongue out and stick it up his ass. Then he dropped him to the floor right before the flunky passed out. The flunky was trying to catch his breath in a pool of his own piss as Chuck stepped over him and continued discussing the plan. That incident, along with other jailhouse stories, solidified Chuck's position in the hood and everyone feared him. Well, mostly everyone…

Chuck approached Keem. They gave each other dap and a hug.

"Welcome back home, my nigga. When did you get out?"

"About nine months ago."

"Damn, that long, nigga? Scoot failed to mention that." Keem looked at Scoot, who was avoiding eye contact with him.

"Yeah; I told that nigga to keep his mouth closed and keep my shit low-key. I wanted niggas to look like they saw a ghost when they saw me."

"Is that right?" Keem said with a smirk on his face.

I sat in the corner, shaking my head, thinking about how lucky I was that I'd dodged a bullet and left this ninja alone when I had. He was more so a clown than a ghost. I must have laughed out loud at my own thoughts, because at that moment, Chuck noticed me sitting in the corner.

"What's up, Re? How're you doing?"

"I'm good," was all I could muster up to say, dryly.

"Damn, you not gonna ask a nigga how I'm doing?"

"How are you doing, Chuck?"

"I'm good, but would be better if I could get back with you."

"That's what's up."

"That's all you got to say?"

"What else you want me to say, Chuck?"

"I want you to say, we can work on us, or you'll think about it or something."

"Nah, I'm straight on that. We're good like we are."

There were a few chuckles in the room. I think Chuck had forgotten there was a house full of people watching us like they were a live audience and we were *The Young and the Restless*, including Keem. He seemed extremely interested, especially in my response. For a moment, we caught each other's eye. He took a sip of Hennessey from the red cup and smirked. I must have held his gaze too long because Chuck grabbed me out the chair by my arm.

"Let me holla at you outside."

I tried to wiggle out of his grip, but to no avail. I was being pulled outdoors.

"YOU'RE HURTING MY ARM! LET ME GO!" I screamed when we got outside.

"Who the fuck is you hollering at? You'd better watch your mouth before I fuck you up."

"Nah, nigga. Your ass better not put your hands on me again, unless you want to take your ass back to jail. I gave your ass a pass last time because I didn't want to contribute to putting another black man behind bars, but try me again if you want to, and I'm calling the po-po on your ass with the quickness."

"Oh, it's like that?"

"Straight like that, nigga."

"So, we're over? You not rocking with me anymore?"

"No; you're cool and all, but I'm not down for the struggle. You need to get a job and stop all that grimy shit you're doing in these streets."

"What the hell are you talking about?"

"I don't have to spell it out. You know what you're out here doing."

"Don't worry about what I'm doing; that's none of your business."

"You know what? You are exactly right. Do you. Bye." I tried walking away.

He grabbed me by my arm again. "I'm not done talking to you."

"But I'm done talking to you. LET! MY! ARM! GO!" I screamed.

He raised his hand to slap the shit out of me as Keem walked out the house. I wasn't sure if he was standing by the doorway listening the whole time.

"Is there a problem?" he asked.

"Not your problem," said Chuck.

"Actually, it is my problem. Especially if she's asking you to let her go and you still have your hand on her arm. Looks like you were ready to hit her." He chuckled but never broke his gaze with Chuck. "Let her arm go."

"Oh, this you now, nigga? This your bitch?" Chuck asked as he let my arm go.

"Who are you calling a bitch?" I said, although I was totally ignored by both parties.

Keem walked closer to Chuck, looked him dead in his eyes and said, "Nah, this ain't my bitch, but she will be my woman. I'm gonna say this only one time, my nigga:

Don't ever put your hand on her again. In fact, don't ever speak to her again. I don't care if y'all are in the same room with each other, don't ever look at her again. Do you understand me?"

There was a moment of silence, and I wasn't sure if Keem was expecting a silenced Chuck to answer him.

Keem, once again never breaking eye contact with Chuck, yelled my name.

"SHEREE!"

Startled, I answered, "Umm, yeah?"

"Don't ever speak to this nigga again. I don't care if y'all in the same room, you look the other way. He doesn't deserve your conversation or your presence. Do you understand me?"

I wanted to scream out, *"YES, DADDY, I UNDERSTAND,"* but all I managed to get out was, "Okay."

Keem extended his hand to me as he continued to look at Chuck.

"Let's go back inside. You don't have to worry about my nigga anymore. He's good."

I took Keem's hand and followed him back in the house.

I'd never had anyone stand up for me before.

Not my father.

Not my brothers.

Not my uncles.

Not even Menard.

It felt so good to feel... protected! When he led me back inside, I felt something I'd never felt before: secure and safe. The type of security and safety you feel when someone wraps their arms around you and shields you from the cold. The monsters. The molesters. The abusers—you know, the assholes of the world. I knew at that moment he would be my everything, and I would be forever grateful for him for saving me from getting the piss slapped out of me by Chuck.

Chuck never came back inside that day. I guess he was too embarrassed. I did see him at Lolo and Scoot's house several times after the incident with his new girlfriend, but he didn't approach me again.

~ Three ~

Sheree

Days turned into months. Keem and I were spending a lot of time together. We didn't really talk much about our relationships because we were each other's escape from them. I couldn't speak about what was going on in his "situationship", but mine was hella complicated. We didn't want to waste the time we had together talking about irrelevant shit. At this point, our relationship was still non-sexual. We usually met for drinks, shot pool, played cards, kicked it at the park, hung out at Scoot's, or Keem's family's house.

Keem had asked me to meet him for drinks at one of his favorite restaurants on the outskirts of the city. He was there first, as usual, so he grabbed a table. I was always late. Usually, it was because I miscalculated how much time it took for me to get dressed or the drive to the location of his choice. When I walked through the door, he stood up and greeted me with a hug. He smelled so good; not sure what cologne it was, but it was new to my nostrils. He appeared to be engaged in a heated conversation with his girlfriend.

"Why are you blowing up my phone? I just left the house fifteen minutes ago."

Silence. She was now talking.

"I told you where I was going and what time I would be back."

More silence.

"We can talk about that when I get home. I wish you would stop putting pressure on me."

More silence.

"Yeah, whatever; I will see you when I get home. Bye."

He disconnected the call before she was able to say anything else. He seemed to be in a different mood.

"You good?"

That was a stupid question to ask, but I wanted to break the ice and give him a minute to get whatever it was off his chest so we could get our date back on track. I hadn't driven thirty minutes to sit and watch him mope. It was time for him to speak now or forever hold his peace.

"Yeah, I'm good. Brittany keeps pressuring me to marry her."

He looked up at me. I guess he wanted to see my reaction. I sat there, stone faced on the outside, but on the inside, I felt like I had been gut-punched. I couldn't let him see I was bothered by this. We hadn't even slept together yet, but I was more pissed than he was that she was pressuring him. I took a deep breath and followed his response with questions of my own.

"What's stopping you from marrying her? Don't you love her? She does have three of your kids. If you have no plans of leaving her, you might as well marry her, right?"

'Did I just say that stupid shit? Did those words just come out my mouth?'

Keem looked at me with a puzzled look on his face. He was probably thinking the same thing I was thinking. *'Why would she say some shit like that? I can't believe that came out her mouth.'* But his response was simple.

"Yeah, maybe you're right; maybe I should marry her."

Awkward.

Thank God the waitress came over to take our order although we hadn't had the chance to look at the menu. We ordered two Long Island Ice Teas and asked if she could give us a few more minutes. He was familiar with the restaurant, so I asked him what his recommendation was.

"They have big-ass sandwiches that are good as hell. You like spicy food like me, so let's start off with some wings and mini-tacos."

"Sounds good to me. Are the wings really hot?"

"Fuck yeah, but we can order the sauce on the side."

"Okay, that's cool."

The wings were hot as hell! I was so glad he'd opted to have the sauce on the side. My upper lip was on fire from the heat of the sauce. I excused myself to go to the bathroom. I had to soak a paper towel in cold water to apply to my lip to get some relief.

For the next few hours, we sat and discussed everything, from relationships to travel. We took turns putting money in the jukebox, testing each other's taste in music, shot a few games of pool, and ordered more drinks. We were having such a good time that we didn't realize it was closing time. Neither one of us was ready to leave, so we sat in my car and listened to some more music.

The music, drinks, and being near each other made us both very horny. We began to kiss and feel on one another. I unbuckled his pants as he reached under my skirt. He pushed my panties to the side and entered my vagina with one finger. I exhaled and stroked his already-hard penis, noticing it was slightly curved. I couldn't take it anymore. My juices were flowing down my leg as he touched all the correct spots. Thankfully, I was parked in a secluded area of the parking lot, away from other cars and the bright streetlights.

With the help of Keem, I wiggled out of my panties and straddled him. He was barely able to get his pants down. I think my juices slid down his penis before I did. He felt so good, like we were meant for each other. Like a hand to a glove. He guided my body to move with his by placing his hands on my ass cheeks. He moved me forward and backward, and up and down.

I had never felt this type of chemistry with anyone else. The energy and electricity we produced together could have lit up a small power plant. He sucked and squeezed my breasts as I rode his dick like I owned it. I told him his dick belonged to me from now on, and my pussy belonged to him going forward. It didn't matter about each other's relationships because this moment right here declared what we were to each other. The mixture of our bodily fluids made us one. Once we climaxed together, we were united. No one could break us.

~ Four ~

Rakeem

I woke up the next morning with a banging-ass headache. The night before was foggy as hell. I looked at the time and noticed it was almost noon. I was supposed to be at the gym an hour ago, but knew I was in no condition to go. Was I dreaming last night? Or had Sheree and I really got down in the parking lot of The Tempting Torpedo? My sac felt empty as if I had sex, but hell, I could have come home and gotten some ass from Brittany.

"Oh, I see you're finally awake. You didn't get home until three a.m."

Guess that answered my question. If I had come home and dicked Brittany down, she wouldn't be talking shit right now. I could come home at eight in the morning and if I broke her off, she would be satisfied I wasn't out giving this D to anyone else.

Completely ignoring her sarcastic comment, I said. "Good morning. Can you bring me an aspirin and some water, Brit?"

"Get it yourself. I know you heard me."

"Heard what?"

"I said you didn't get home until three a.m."

"I heard you, but it was a statement, not a question, so I didn't think it warranted a response."

"Yeah, okay; I see you're starting that bullshit again. Let me find out your ass is out there fucking around. We're going to have a real fucking problem in this bitch."

"Girl, move out my way. I don't have time for this shit. My head is pounding and you're talking about me coming in at three in the morning, like it's something I do on a regular basis. I can see if I was doing this shit every night, but I'm not. I go to the city once or twice a month. Other than that, I'm in this damn house. Hell, I think I'm going to start getting out more. I need to get away from your nagging ass."

"Yeah, okay. Next time you want to hang out in the city, you can take the kids with you. They haven't seen your momma and them in a minute. I'm about to go the store."

"Yeah, okay."

After taking the pills, I jumped in the shower. I tried my best to remember last night, but some areas were still a blur. I didn't remember everything, but I couldn't forget that I had been inside one of the tightest pussies I had ever been in. I have had sex with females of all nationalities, but I put Sheree up there with my top two. That number-one spot goes to a white chick from Flint named Izzy, short for Elizabeth, I use to fuck with when I was selling drugs. Her pussy was good, but her head was phenomenal! They should have called that bitch Bissell because she could suck a bowling ball through a straw. I could never be with her for real for real because she was just a pass-around for me and my homies. Thinking about Izzy had my dick hard as a brick.

I shook that shit off and went back to trying to recollect last night events. If Sheree's head game matched her pussy game, I was gonna be like dude on Harlem Nights. Sunshine's pussy was so good that he'd called home, spoken to his child, *then* asked to speak to his wife. He told her ass he was never coming home. I loved the fact that she could get freaky in the middle of a parking lot. That shit was daring and exciting as fuck! Anyone could have walked up on us at any time—departing customers, staff, or the police!

Thinking about that made my already-hard dick swell even more. I found myself caressing my soapy dick with my right hand as I balanced myself on the wall of the shower with the left one. The hot, steamy water running down my back felt so good, and I continued to caress my dick with the silky shea butter body wash. It felt so good and wet—like Sheree's pussy.

'The way she'd grinded back and forth slowly on my dick was magical. If I remembered correctly, she was moving to the beat of her playlist that was filled with slow, seductive melodies. Our bodies were in perfect harmony as I inhaled the breath she exhaled. I knew she was ready to climax as she moved faster and faster. Her arms around my neck got tighter and tighter.'

Then something happened. I remembered it now! *'She tightened her pussy muscles and started moving up and down with so much force her pussy started to make farting noises and I started to lose it. I couldn't take it anymore. I was about to explode and so was she. We were now looking in each other in the eyes. Time seemed to stand still. She was still grinding up and down on me, but it seemed to be in slow motion. She moved closer to* me and told me this dick belonged to her and her pussy belonged to me.'

I was totally gone in the moment when I felt that feeling last night. My body started to jerk as I grunted. I felt so relieved as I watched my semen go down the drain. I felt alive, young, and refreshed. The headache was gone and I was ready to start a new day. I had an extra pep in my step and an extra glide in my stride. I got out the shower and checked my phone. Obviously, Sheree had had a good time as well because she had texted me several times:

Sheree: Good morning Sunshine! Rise and shine!

Sheree: Hey big head! Lol

Sheree: Damn, someone must have given you some of that Nyquil, muscle relaxer, *Ill Na-Na*! Get at me when you wake up.

I laughed at the last message out loud before responding.

Keem: Good afternoon Sweetie. I'm finally getting myself together. Someone MUST HAVE given me some Nyquil, muscle-relaxer-ass, *Ill Na-Na*, because I was in a coma. How are you doing this afternoon?

Sheree: I'm fine and I feel great! I guess I have you to thank for that huh?

Keem: Nah, ma, that was all you. I did nothing but enjoy the ride. You were in your element

	last night. I can only imagine what you could do with extra time and space.
Sheree:	Why do you have to imagine when you can find out whenever you want?
Keem:	Don't threaten me with a good time. But this time, I will do the driving. I can't let you one-up me again. You took me by surprise. Hell, you raped me! Lol
Sheree:	And you liked it...nope you loved it. I bet you want me to "rape" you again huh?
Keem:	Maybe.
Sheree:	I don't like that word. Say it.
Keem:	Say what?
Sheree:	Say you want me to rape you. Say you want me to take that D.
Keem:	Lol, girl. You are tripping.
Sheree:	Say that you want some more of me Keemie.
Keem:	I want some more of you Sweetie.
Sheree:	Cool! Meet me at the Econo Lodge on Michigan Ave in an hour. Let me know the room number.

What the fuck had I gotten myself into? I was looking at the text, unsure of how to respond. Should I go and tear that ass up? Or should I chill? I was already in the doghouse; maybe I shouldn't push it. But, then again, I had just rubbed one off, so I could probably fuck the shit out of her for a long time. Fuck it! I was going. I replied to her message.

Keem: Ok.

I arrived at the hotel and checked in. I wasn't too worried about being seen because Brittany had very few friends and the hotel was in a predominantly-white neighborhood. I paid cash for the room and texted Sheree the room number.

I wasn't sure why I was nervous. She and I had just had sex last night. Today, I was sober, so I couldn't use being drunk as an excuse. Just as I started to get settled in the room, my cellphone went off and it was Brittany. She must have either made it home or was on her way. I already had my lie planned, so I answered the phone.

"Hello."

"Where are you?"

Which meant she was home.

"Tone had an emergency and needed me to come through for a minute."

"What kind of emergency, Keem?"

"I'm not about to go into that man's business with you. Just know that he needed me, so I had to pull up. I'll be back in a few hours."

"What kind of problem does he have that warrants you being gone for a few hours? We have problems here that need to be addressed."

"No, we don't have problems that need to be addressed. *You* have a problem you want to address with me. There's a difference."

"If I have a problem with you, then it becomes our problem, and it needs to be addressed!"

"Yeah, well, it won't be getting addressed at this moment, so if you don't have anything else you want to talk about, I will see you in a few hours."

"Whatever; don't be gone all night."

"And don't tell me what to do or not to do."

"Whatever; bye."

"Bye."

I sent Tone a quick text to tell him, that if asked, I was with him and I would explain later. Shortly after sending the text, there was a knock on the door. I got off the bed and looked out the peephole to see Sheree standing there. Although I knew it was her, I still asked, "Who is it?" She looked directly in the peep hole and said, "I know you see me. Open this door."

I opened the door and stepped aside so she could walk in. It was now fall, so she had on a light jacket, skintight jeans, and tall, brown riding boots that hugged her firm legs. She placed a brown paper bag on the table. The only things I could see sticking out the top of the bag were two red cups. She said hello as she removed her North Face jacket to show off a cute, fuzzy mocha-brown sweater with a plunging neckline. Her breasts stood at attention. I couldn't take my eyes off them. Last night, when we'd had sex, nothing was removed but the bottom half of our clothes. I hadn't gotten the pleasure of looking at her body like I'd wanted to.

"Hello," I managed to say.

As she walked over to me, I couldn't help but admire how sexy she was. Her hair was now in a messy bun standing on top of her head. Her face was glowing from the Clinique moisturizer and foundation mix she used that gave her a skin a more-natural and cleaner look, instead of the made-up look a lot of the females were going for these days. Her lips were full, plump, extra glossy, and matched the color of her sweater. If I had given her a kiss at that moment, I'm sure my lips would have slid from hers with barely a touch.

She gave me hug. I immediately smelled the mixture of a freshly-showered body with a hint of cucumber melon. She gave me a long kiss on the lips. I stood there taking in all of her. The smell of her lip gloss, chocolate. The smell of her hair, coconut and shea butter. And the smell of her breath, a minty peppermint. Not sure if it was gum or toothpaste, but it was fresh.

I grabbed her by her waist and moved my hand up and down her lower back. She tried to pull away, but I wasn't having it. I wanted her now. I removed her sweater. She had on the prettiest lace bra. I gently pushed her on the bed and removed my shirt, exposing my ripped stomach. I worked out five times a week: weights, cardio, and calisthenics. I paid extra attention to my stomach and legs. Sit ups and squats were a must. The sit ups did my stomach justice, but the squats only worked on my legs, not much for my butt. No matter what I tried, no muscles were being distributed there. Still flat as fuck, but I'm a dude, so it wasn't a big concern. Wasn't like a nigga was gonna go get implants or nothing. I just wanted a little something extra to help support my gun and holster.

I could tell she was impressed by my abs by the way she kept staring at them. I flexed my chest muscles a little, just to give her a show. She chuckled as I finished undressing, exposing another part of my body that was also rock hard. She bit her lip and leaned back on her elbows, taking all of me in. I removed her boots and socks, exposing her pedicured feet with black toenail polish. I moved upward and kissed her belly button before unbuttoning her jeans and pulling them down. She assisted by wiggling out of them. Her black lace panties and bra were the only thing between us.

I towered over her and just looked in her eyes. She smiled and grabbed the back of my neck and pulled my lips into hers. We kissed for what seemed hours. I was so hard I was about to bust. She must have sensed it because she reached down and grabbed him. She started to caress my dick with her right hand, still holding the back of my neck. She used the pre-cum that had escaped to massage the head of my dick. That shit felt so good that I had to return the favor.

I managed to pull her panties to the side. They were soaking wet. I inserted my finger into her wet volcano and almost came on the spot! It was so wet and warm. I felt her pussy throbbing on my finger. I inserted another one, and she gasped for air and bit her lip. We were stroking each other in harmony, trying to see who would explode first. She lost. Her legs began to tighten and shake. She let go of my dick and gripped the sheets. I took that opportunity to dive in. I purposely rubbed my dick up and down her clit twice before ramming my dick inside her and keeping it there. She screamed out and tightened up, which put my dick at her mercy. I whispered in her ear for her to relax and she exhaled, which loosened her grip of my dick.

I moved in and out of her real slow. I wanted her to feel every inch of me. I was in complete control and I wanted her to know that. Last night, she had caught me off guard, but today, she was gonna pay for it. I paid attention to her facial expressions each time I went in and out of her. I wanted to see which movement made her cringe. Made her smile. Made her bite her lip. Made her stick her nails into my skin. I was gonna use all of that to my advantage every chance I got. She grabbed the back of my ass and gestured for me to go faster. When I didn't respond, she became vocal.

"Faster, Keemie."

"Say please."

"NO!"

I stopped in mid-stroke. "Say please."

"Stop playing," she whined.

"I'm not playing; say please!"

I started to move in and out of her at the pace of a locomotive just starting its route. She was losing it. The hook that I'd thought was abnormal as a young child was now the hook and sinker to all the women I'd had the pleasure of sexin'.

"Pleeeeaaaasssseeee!" she whined.

"Please what?" I whispered in her ear.

"Please go faster!"

"I can't hear you," I said as I picked up the pace just a little.

"FUCK ME FASTER!" she screamed.

"Say please!" I demanded as I rammed my dick inside her with force.

"PLEASE FUCK ME FASTER, KEEMIE!" she screamed.

As soon as she said that, I picked up the pace, gently grabbing her by her neck as I kissed her lips. She was panting like she was out of breath as she dug her nails in my back. This made me more aggressive. I loosened the grip around her neck and lifted her leg, placed it on my shoulder, and leaned forward. This pushed her leg closer to her own shoulder. I started long-stroking her. Her eyes bucked. She opened her mouth to say something but couldn't get the words out. I covered her mouth with mine and dove in even deeper.

Her sounds became more muffled and her legs began to shake. I removed my mouth from hers and looked down at her. She appeared to be in a paralyzed state of shock as her whole body began to shake. She tried to push me away, but I wasn't finished. I was yet to cum and I wasn't done making her cum either. I allowed her to push me off her this time. As soon as she started to curl up in a fetal position, I grabbed her leg and flipped her on her stomach. She tried to crawl away, but I grabbed her around her waist.

"Where do you think you're going?"

"Nooooo! I can't take anymore, Keemie!" she whined.

"Oh, yes, you can."

I straddled her from behind and parted her legs by using one of mine. I pushed her head into the pillows, positioned her ass upward, and entered her from behind.

She gripped the covers and let the pillow muffle her scream. I pounded in and out of her pussy like I was a dying man and this pussy was my last wish. She screamed my name as I forced myself deep inside her. I grabbed her by her shoulder to lift her. Then she did the unthinkable. She began to grunt and throw that pussy back at me. That shit felt so good! I had to slow her down so I wouldn't explode, but that didn't stop her. She pushed backward and was in an upright position.

We were no longer in a doggie-style position. I was sitting on my feet and she was bouncing on my shit. I grabbed her by her breasts and let her continue to take advantage of me. I was tired as a ma'fucka anyway and I could use the down time to catch my breath. She continued to bounce on my dick as I sucked her neck and squeezed her breasts. She put her hands on top of mine as if to gesture for me to squeeze her breasts harder, so I did.

She began to buck uncontrollably. I could sense she was ready to cum again, so I had to regain control. I pushed her back down and grabbed her by her bun. Her hair slipped out the ponytail holder, but that didn't stop me. I grabbed a fistful of it and started fucking the shit out her. She screamed like I was killing her, but I didn't care. She started bucking back.

"Take this pussy, daddy!"

Why did she have to go and say that?! I started to go faster and harder as her flow matched mine.

"I'M ABOUT TO COME, KEEMIE!"

"You're about to come for daddy?"

"Yes, daddy! Please come with me!"

And just like that, my dick turned on me and started to listen to her.

"I'm about to come with you, sweetie. Give me this pussy, baby.'

"It's yours, daddy. Take it!"

That's all I needed to hear. Hers legs began to tighten and my heart began to race, and like a volcano, I erupted. All my lava shot like a rocket into Sheree. Once again, we became one. As I exhaled, Sheree jumped off my still-erect dick and put it in her mouth. She began to suck me dry. I grabbed her head to remove her, but she wouldn't let up. So, I sat there shaking like I had a seizure disorder as she sucked my soul out of me.

After she was done, she lay back on the bed, grinning and satisfied like a vampire who had just experienced their first taste of blood. She wiped her mouth with the back of her hand and said, "Do you want something to drink?"

All I could do was look at her like she was crazy and nod. Did this chick know she'd just suck my larynx out my dick hole?? She'd just made everything I'd done today look mediocre with that chess move she'd just pulled. I was a pawn in her game, and she was the queen. I was in deep thought. She'd only had her mouth on my dick for one minute. If that was just a snippet of what her head game was like, then I was in really big trouble.

"Keem!" I heard her say.

"What's up?"

"A penny for your thoughts."

"Oh, nothing; just wondering what I'm going to eat for dinner."

"Is that right?" She looked at me like she didn't believe a word I'd said.

"Yep."

"Want to order a pizza or something? I've got time to chill if you do."

The correct answer would be to say no, but I couldn't. I wasn't ready to leave her. Even if I wanted to, my legs were noodles, so I couldn't.

"That's what's up. I don't like anchovies, pineapples, or mushrooms."

"I don't like anchovies or pineapples either. Mushrooms, I'll spare you this time. Banana or jalapeno peppers?"

"Don't matter; the hotter the better. Get some hot wings as well."

"Sounds good to me. I'll place the order. Here… drink up." She handed me a drink.

I took the drink and shook my head. Damn, I done fucked up.

~ Five ~

Sheree

The last few days were amazing! I had experienced something I hadn't experienced in a long time—butterflies in my stomach. By now, Menard and I were back together, but I was sure it was out of familiarity and convenience more than anything else. Don't get me wrong, we loved each other, but somewhere along the way, we'd fallen out of love with each other. We had been so on-and-off since we were teenagers that we thought being on-and-off was the norm. We had two kids together, twins, a boy and a girl, but they were of age and able to fend for themselves. We turned a blind eye to each other's bullshit—unless it was blatantly in the open or outright disrespectful. Then it had to be addressed. I knew he was doing his own thing, but I didn't give a damn because I was having fun doing me. Fair exchange is no robbery.

Keem and I had crossed the threshold that could never be undone. We'd had sex! Powerful sex! I'd thought the energy in the car had been electrifying and amazing, but it was nothing compared to what I'd experienced the previous night. My dumb ass had had the nerve to initiate the rendezvous, thinking I would have the upper hand like I'd had at the Tempting Torpedo. Man, was I wrong! Keem seemed prepared to take back the throne! He was in straight-up beast mode that night! The way he'd taken charge alone had me climbing the walls. I'd never had a man so vocal in the bedroom. Damn, I love that shit.

Orgasm after orgasm was what I'd experienced. Just when I'd thought he was done, because I surely had been, he'd flipped me on my stomach and fucked the shit out of me! He was able to be gentle but aggressive, demanding but giving. I hadn't wanted to pull out my secret weapon so soon, but he'd left me no choice. He'd dicked me down and had me begging for the D on some desperate shit! I had never sucked a dude's dick after they'd cum before, but I'd watched pornos from time to time and noticed when the girls did it, it drove the men crazy. So, I'd tried it. Mission accomplished! He thought he'd had the last hurrah until I gave him a little Super Head action. I'm not a one-trick pony. I've got great pussy and extraordinary head. What I'd given him was just enough to keep him wondering. If he didn't come back for anything else, I knew he'd come back for the full-course meal after receiving the appetizer I'd given him.

After we were done, I'd had to have something to drink and eat. I was parched from screaming like a maniac and hungry from sweating out the calories I'd consumed earlier in the day. Before coming to the room, I'd purchased a bottle of Crown Royal, a coke, and an energy drink. The energy drink was for him. Now I saw why he mixed his drink with a Red Bull. That shit really does give you wings!

We ordered pizza, got drunk, and talked for a few more hours. It was getting late and both our phones were jumping, Menard for me and Brittany for him. Once again, neither one of us wanted to part ways, but we had to get back to civilization. But not before trying to have one more rendezvous. Although we both had eaten, we were still hungry for each other. However, we couldn't move past first base. His phone was blowing up. He'd informed me that Brittany was pissed he'd come in late the previous night. Leaving out the house like he had added to the fire.

I'd wanted to convince him to stay, but I needed to get home as well. Menard wasn't on me as hard as Brittany was; he just wanted to know how long I would be out. I wasn't sure if it was out of concern, being nosy, or if he was using it to gauge how long he would have to hang out with his "friends". Keem and I had parted ways with a promise we would meet up again later in the week. I'd packed up the remainder of the drink, ate another slice of pizza, and we'd exited the hotel.

On the drive home, I'd received a phone call from Jackson, one of the twins.

"Ma, what time are you coming home?"

"I'm on way home now, Jack; what's up?"

"I'm hungry."

"Well, go in the kitchen and fix something to eat."

"There's nothing to eat in there; I checked."

"Don't you mean there's nothing *you* want to eat in there?"

Silence.

"What do y'all want to eat? And where is your sister?"

"It doesn't matter. She's on the phone."

"It does matter, because if I pick up some food and y'all don't eat it, there's going to be a problem."

My line beeped; it was Keem.

"Go talk to your sister and come to an agreement about what y'all want to eat and call me back. And I'm only stopping at one place. I'm about twenty minutes out."

"Okay, Ma. Call you back in a minute."

I clicked over to Keem.

"Hello, stranger. Are you almost home?"

"Not quite; I had to stop and pick up the kids a pizza."

"How ironic is that? We just had pizza." We laughed.

"I know, right? Now I have to pretend to be hungry."

He laughed again.

"Yeah, I told my demon seeds to call me back once they've decided what they want. Speaking of the devils, this is one of them now. Hold on for a minute."

This time it was my daughter calling.

"Hey, Journee. Did y'all decide what y'all want to eat?"

"Hey, Ma; yes. We ordered a pizza from Cottage Inn. It will be ready in twenty minutes."

"Great! Sounds good." I tried to sound enthused as I rolled my eyes. "I will be there shortly. Any surprises?"

"Yes; we ordered wings and a Coke with it too. See you when you get here. Love you!"

"Love you too; bye."

I clicked back over to Keem.

"Sorry about that. You aren't going to believe what they want to eat."

"Pizza?"

"Yes; how ironic is that. Guess, you aren't the only who has to act like you're hungry for pizza tonight." I laughed.

"Guess not. Hold one sec, I just pulled up to this pizza joint and I'm about to walk in. Or would you prefer I call you back?"

"I can hold."

"Okay."

I heard him inform the employee he was picking up an order for Rakeem. Meanwhile, my song came on the radio. Nelly and Kelly Rowland's *Dilemma*. I started to sing.

Baby I love you / And I need you / Nelly I love you, I do / Need you.
No matter what I do / All I think about is you / Even when I'm with my boo / Boy you know I'm crazy over you...

Keem came back to the phone. "Oh, that's how you really feel about a nigga, huh?"

"Yep, that's how I really feel about Nelly." I laughed.

"Shiddd, Nelly ain't got shit on me… outside of the money."

"You're right, babe; he ain't got shit on you."

"Say that again."

"Say what again?"

"Call me babe again."

"No! Why?"

"Because I like the way you say it."

"Babe."

"Say it like you mean that shit."

There he went with that taking charge shit I love so much, and I did what I was told.

"Babe, you trippin."

"That's what I'm talking about. From this point forward, that's how I want you to refer to me. I'm your 'babe'."

I chuckled like a schoolgirl. "Okay, and going forward, you're to refer to me as sweetie, deal?"

"Bet, sweetie."

"Yes, just like that."

"Okay, *sweetie*. I just pulled up to the house. Text me later if you can."

"Okay, babe. Love you."

'Fuck! Did I just say that out loud?? Please tell me I didn't say that out loud.'

There was complete silence on the other end of the phone. I wondered if he was still there or if he'd hung up. Maybe he hadn't heard that part. Maybe he'd hung up beforehand. I looked at the phone. Nope, he was still there. Out of embarrassment, I hit end on the call.

I punched the hell out the steering wheel several times out of frustration and embarrassment. Frustrated at myself for letting those words slip out my mouth for any other man but Menard. Embarrassment because of his lack of response. Or even worse, he didn't feel the same way I felt. I didn't remember stopping at the Cottage Inn, but I was pulling in the driveway with the pizza, wings, and a pop in my hand. Thank God Menard wasn't home. I felt so guilty suddenly. Not because I was cheating with Keem, but because I'd said I love you to another man. The kids bombarded me for the food.

"Mom, do you want any?" asked Jackson.

"No, you guys go ahead. Suddenly, I don't feel too good. I'm going to bed."

"Okay, Ma; feel better. Good night," Journee said.

"Good night, you two. Clean up your mess when you're done. Love you guys; good night."

Even saying good night to the kids sounded different.

I headed to my room, removed my clothes, and jumped in the shower. I wished I could forget those words, wished they would just go down the drain. The shower was the perfect place to end the night. I loved taking showers when I got off work. It helped relieve and wash away work-related stress. I usually got out feeling refreshed and rejuvenated. I was hoping for the same this night. I was hoping I could erase those three words from my vocabulary and forget I'd ever said them to Keem.

It didn't work.

I turned off my phone, took two Tylenol PM's, and jumped in bed. As I lay on my back, I looked at the ceiling, thinking about the day's events that had led to the night's emotions. Had I fallen in love with Keem? That couldn't be happening. Not like that. Not that soon. Not under these conditions. A single tear fell from my eye. I let it fall as I closed my eyes. Thankfully, sleep came sooner than later. I was mentally drained and sleep was the only escape.

~ Six ~

Rakeem

I had been trying to reach Sheree for several days, to no avail. It appeared she was dodging my calls and ignoring my text messages. I knew she was probably a little perplexed that I hadn't responded when she'd said she loved me the other day. It wasn't that I didn't love her, because I did. It was just that I had been caught off guard. Probably because I hadn't told Sheree that Brittany and I had gotten married. I didn't know why I was scared to tell her. After all, she was the one who'd told me to marry her. Even though we both were in other relationships, I did love Sheree. Brittany and I had kids together, and she had been down since we were teenagers. It was only right that I'd made an honest woman out of her. After all, she did say to marry her, right?

My phone started to ring. It was Scoot.

"What's up, fool?"

"Nothing, my nigga; what's going on?"

"Shit, trying to get in contact with Sheree, but she keeps dodging me."

"Really? Lolo talked to her yesterday."

"Straight up? Did you hear what they were talking about?"

"Nah, man; I wasn't listening to their girly conversation."

"Shit! Did you tell Lolo that Brittany and I got married?"

"Maaaan, I may have mentioned it to her; I don't know."

"Nigga, what do you mean, you don't know?! Did you tell her ass or not?!"

"Yeah, man, I mentioned it. I didn't know it was a secret, nigga! You haven't told Sheree?"

"No, fuck, man! I hope Lolo hasn't told her. I need to tell her before Lolo opens her big mouth. Is Lolo there?"

"Yeah; she's in the other room."

"Ask her if she told Sheree I married Brittany."

"Hold on," Scoot said as he asked Lolo.

"She said no, she didn't tell her, but she said Sheree didn't sound like herself."

"Okay, bet. I need you to have Lolo make up a reason to get Sheree over to your house. Set it up and get back at me with the day and time."

"Okay, my nigga. I'll text you when it's done."

"Bet."

I hung up the phone and tried to call Sheree one more time. No answer. Brittany walked in the room.

"Hey, husband! What're you up to?"

"Nothing. Just got off the phone with Scoot. What's up?"

"I want to go hang out with the girls for a few hours. You mind watching the kids for a bit?"

"That's cool. Go ahead."

"Thanks, babe. Let me get dressed."

I nodded my head and checked my phone to see if Sheree had called back or responded to any of my text messages. Nothing.

I turned on the TV in the family room, grabbed my headset, and turned on *Call of Duty*. It temporarily took my mind off my problems. Nothing like shooting people down while talking shit. Usually, I whooped ass on this game, but not today. These ma'fuckas were picking me off left and right. I couldn't concentrate for shit. I knew it was time to turn the game off when I started taking the trash-talking on the other end of the headphones personally.

I turned off the game and surfed the sixty-five inch for a good show to watch. I decided to watch the *Martin* marathon on TBS. Nothing like a good laugh to make you feel better. I checked the guide to see if I'd missed my favorite episode. I loved the *Nino Brown* episode. When Martin dragged that fake-ass dog around and across the table, I always fell out laughing. The episode was scheduled to come in a couple of hours. Although I'd watched the episode many times, I taped it just in case I got busy and missed it. My phone started to ring. It was Scoot.

"What's up?"

"Sheree will be here in an hour."

"An hour? Damn, man, I got the kids."

Brittany had left thirty minutes ago.

"Aye, man, I did what you asked."

"You're right, bro; good looking out. I will try to be there in an hour. Don't let her leave; I have to get these kids together."

"Okay, gotcha. See you soon."

I called out to the kids, "RJ, Neisha, Rayne! Go wash up and put on your clothes. We're going to see Grandma."

The kids yelled in unison. They were happy to go see my mother because they hadn't seen her in a while. As they got dressed, lots of thoughts went through my mind. I shot Brittany a text to let her know I was headed to my mom's house with the kids. During that time, I checked to see if I'd missed any calls or had any unopened messages from Sheree. Still no luck. I hurried the kids along as I got dressed. I stopped at McDonald's to make sure they were fed and out the way. I also stopped at the store to grab a pint of Crown Royal and a Red Bull for me, and snacks and juices for the kids. As we drove down I-94, I gave them my usual speech.

"When we get to your grandmother's house, y'all had better behave. No running in and out the house. No begging for anything, because y'all have already eaten and have plenty of snacks. No fighting with each other or with the other kids."

"What if someone hits me first?" asked RJ, as always.

"RJ, if someone hits you *first*, you have every right and my permission to hit them back. That doesn't mean fight, that means hit them back. If the person is adamant about picking a fight with you, then you whoop their ass. Understand?"

"Got it, Dad," RJ responded.

"Does everybody understand?"

"Yeeees!" they all said in unison.

The ride down I-94 was bumpy as always. Winter was approaching and the roads were starting to crumble. The City of Detroit, as usual, had just patched up the potholes. They seemed oblivious to the fact, that as drivers drove over the filled potholes, they eventually unfilled. We approached our Chalmers exit, and I informed the kids to gather their things.

We pulled up to my mom's house on Lakewood and Chandler Park Drive. The neighborhood was still in pretty-good shape. Most of the neighbors owned their homes, so they took pride into keeping them up. There were Neighborhood Block Association signs posted on the corner of almost every street along Chandler Park Drive. This was an indicator to warn people that the neighbors stood in solidarity and kept a watchful eye on crime in the area. Each block association had a president, vice president, and secretary. Treasurers were few, due to mishandling of funds and a lack of trust. As a result, the majority of the block clubs had decided to collect funds on a "need-to-do-so" basis.

Homeowners held themselves accountable and responsible for vacant lots next to their property. They cut the grass and trimmed the trees as well as picked up trash. This encouraged them to purchase the lots if they were for sale or became available. Some rebuilt on their new land, while others installed privacy fences to add to their home or extend their backyards. They had yearly competitions on the best-kept yards. This forced the kids to play on the sidewalk or in one of the fields located on the block. Playing on the grass on this street led to repercussions and consequences.

We pulled up to Mom's house and the kids jumped out the car. She was sitting on her enclosed porch, sipping on a glass of Riunite Lambrusco wine. She had the bottle hidden behind the table. My mom was very "bougghetto", bougie and ghetto. She was of average height, light-brown skin, with sandy-brown, shoulder-length hair. She had a small frame, except for her large breasts. When she leaned forward, it looked like she would fall over because they were so big. No one messed with my mama because they knew she was crazy. She could crack you in the head with a bottle without spilling the contents. I have seen her cuss plenty of ma'fuckas out with her legs crossed and pinky finger extended as she sipped on a cup of tea.

The kids opened the screen door and ran into their grandmother's arms.

"How are my grandbabies doing?"

"Fiiiiiine!" they said in unison.

"Y'all hungry?"

They looked at me. I gave them that look.

"No; we just ate," Rayne said.

I gave her an approving nod and a smile.

"How are you doing, Son?"

"I'm good, Ma. How are you?"

"I'm okay. Your damn sisters are getting on my nerves, Toni with her damn kids and Tonya acting an ass in school. She is smart as hell, but that attitude is going to stop colleges from recruiting her."

Rotoni was one year younger than I was. She had four kids with her ex-boyfriend, Butch. He was currently doing two years for a crime he said he didn't commit, which might have been true in his eyes. His friend Gerald had asked him to run him to the store. Butch had stayed in the car. He'd had no idea Gerald was planning to rob the store. When Gerald came out, he noticed Gerald didn't have anything in his hand and he was sweating like crazy. He asked Gerald what happened, and Gerald responded they didn't have what he wanted. Butch didn't think anything else as he drove away.

Surveillance cameras placed near the vicinity of the store had caught Gerard getting into Butch's car. They had been able to trace the car back to Butch by getting a read on the license plate. Butch had refused to give Gerard up. He had been charged with being an accessory to the robbery. Those charges had been dropped because the owner couldn't pick him out of a line up. However, it still had been a violation of his probation, so he had to do the remaining time on the old charge. He was hoping to get time reduced for good behavior. He was almost at the halfway mark.

Rotoni had solely depended on Butch to take care of her and the kids. When Butch got locked up, she had been forced to move back home with Mama until she was able to get a job. She didn't seem to be in a rush, and there was always an excuse. The job was too far. Her car wouldn't make it. She had no one to pick up the kids from school. It didn't pay enough. Or, it paid too much, which would interfere with her welfare benefits. I was waiting for her to use the dog as an excuse any minute. I could imagine her saying, "No one will be home to walk or feed the dog," or "They wouldn't allow me to bring the dog to work. I informed them that he was an emotional support dog."

If Mama allowed it, what was I to say? When she complained about Toni, I would listen, but my answer remained the same. I'd told her Toni only did what she allowed her to do. Mama would cop an attitude, then change the subject. She didn't want to hear that shit I had to say! Lol.

Tonya was the baby girl. Straight-A student at Southeastern High School. She played in all the sports and was very popular among her peers. Like Mama, she was no-nonsense. This caused lots of issues at school. She was quick to go off if provoked. The only reason she never had been expelled was because of her grades. Her teachers and counselor were trying their best to make sure she walked across the stage with the honors she deserved, but she didn't make it easy. She wanted to go to college to be a mechanical engineer, and so far, she had been accepted at five colleges. She hadn't decided if she wanted to go away to college or stay close to home. She was really attached to Mama.

I received a text message from Scoot stating Sheree had arrived. Mama, of course, wanted to make small talk because she hadn't seen me in a while.

"How does it feel to be a married man?"

"The same, I guess."

"I'm surprise you went through with it."

"Oh yeah? Why is that?"

"Although you love her, you don't appear to be *in love* with her."

"She is the mother of my kids, and she has held me down since high school. She deserves the title, don't you think?"

"Maybe she does, but that doesn't mean you had to be the person to give it to her."

"Mama, why are you saying all this right now? Why not say this before I got married?"

"One, because y'all just went and got married without telling anyone. Two, I see how much you care for Sheree."

Sheree and I had met at Mama's house on several occasions, so Mama was aware of our relationship and the feelings I had for her.

"What does Sheree have to do with anything?" I laughed.

"I see the way you look at her. Your entire demeanor changes when you're around her—for that matter, whenever her name is brought up. When speaking to you about Brittany and marriage, you had a somber look on your face. Your shoulders were slumped and your back hunched. When I mentioned Sheree, your posture changed. You stood up straight, like a soldier, and your face brightened up."

She paused for a minute and looked me straight in my eyes. I turned my head to avoid contact.

"You're in love with Sheree!" she yelled.

"Mama, calm down!"

I looked around to see if any of the kids were in earshot. They were like sponges. Anything said and heard was liable to get back to Brittany. I wouldn't be surprised if she questioned the shit out of them when they arrived back home.

"Ain't this some shit! Did you know this before you married Brittany?"

"I don't know. Maybe. It may be just lust. I'm sure you would like it if Sheree and I were to end up together." I laughed, trying to change the subject. "You've never really cared for Brittany."

"It's not that I don't care for her. She just thinks she's better than everyone. Thinks because her family has money, she can look down on us."

When I didn't interject to tell her she was wrong, she continued.

"Sheree is down to earth. She stands her ground with you and takes no shit. She's bossy and assertive. She always brings me wine when she comes over, and most importantly, she's a Leo like me!"

I started laughing. I knew that was the main reason she liked Sheree. Their birthdays were two days apart. Mama and her zodiac signs. Leos could do no wrong in her eyes. They were the first, last, and only sign in her eyes. She possessed all the signs of a Leo: bossy, confident, smart, and tenacious. If she saw something she wanted, she went after it until she got it.

"Okay, Mama, I hear you." I shook my head. "Truthfully, I want to leave the kids here for a few hours. I told Scoot to arrange for Sheree to come over so I can talk to her about something."

"Arrange for her to come over? Why you didn't ask her to come over here?"

"If I did that, she probably wouldn't show up."

"What the hell did you do to her?"

"I didn't do anything to her, Mama." I laughed. "She said something and my lack of response may have made her feel a certain way. Plus, I need to tell her that Brittany and I are married before she finds out from someone else."

"WHAT! SHE STILL DOESN'T KNOW?!"

"No, Ma, I didn't know how to tell her."

"Well, you'd better figure it out quick. And, Son, when a woman tells you she loves you and doesn't get a response, she tends to shut down. She may be a little embarrassed."

I looked at her shocked.

"How do you know that's what she said, Mama?"

"It's a Leo thing. We have psychic powers."

"Okay, Mama. Let me go straighten this out before it gets out of line."

"Okay. Tell Sheree I said hello and to come have a drink with me if it isn't too late."

"Got it, Mama. I love you. See you in a few."

"Love you too. Be careful out there."

I jumped in my car and texted Scoot to inform him I was on my way. I turned on Young Jeezy's *Recession* CD and played my favorite song, *Hustlaz Ambitions*. I turned the music up as far as it would go.

I come so far from the bottom couldn't even see the top
Just as soon as a feel the drought, I'm whippin' up every block
I'm a good God-fearing man with a criminal mind state
Ain't no one gave a shit and that's why we grind weight
My grandma off in the church while I'm in the refrigerator
In search of the baking soda right next to the mashed potatoes
She prayin' for better days, I'm prayin' it take this water

Realest that done this shit put that there on my mother and daughter...

I needed this thug motivation to get me prepared to face Sheree. I wasn't sure how she was going to take the news or where we would go next. I pulled up to the house in ten minutes. Scoot didn't live far from Mama's house, but I had hoped it would take a little longer than usual. I spotted Chuck's black-on-black Chrysler 300 on twenty-fours and Sheree's red Dodge Charger across the street from each other. Jealousy automatically entered my mind.

'Why is this nigga over here? Especially right now?' I didn't need that bullshit. If that nigga was all in my girl's face, we were gonna have a fuckin' problem. I jumped out the car with my gun on my hip, just in case I needed to lay that nigga down.

I walked into the house and spoke to everyone, including Chuck. I felt a sense of relief that he and Sheree weren't in the same room. I didn't see her, but I knew she was close because of the faint smell of the Versace Bright Crystal perfume she loved to wear. Lolo and Sheree walked in the room laughing. She didn't notice me offhand. Whatever they were laughing at had her full attention. When she noticed me, she immediately stopped laughing. She looked at Scoot, Lolo, then me. Everyone seemed to be staring at me.

"Hello, Sheree," I said.

"Hello, Rakeem." She looked me dead in my eyes.

I could tell she was upset. She hadn't called me Rakeem since the first day we'd met. Her glaze was cold and blank. She was looking at me but wasn't really looking at me. She was looking *through* me.

"Can I holler at you for a minute?"

"About?"

"Let me holla at you and I'll tell you."

"Start hollering," she said as she stood back on one leg with her arms folded.

"In private."

She turned around, grabbed her purse, and headed in the direction of Lolo's and Scoot's bathroom.

I followed her in the bathroom, closed and locked the door.

"What do you want to talk to me about, Rakeem?"

"Oh, I'm Rakeem again? What's up with that? I thought we were better than that, sweetie."

"I thought we were too, and don't call me sweetie. What do you want to talk to me about?"

"Straight like that?"

"Yes, straight like that."

"Okay, whatever. First off, I didn't mean to give you the silent treatment when you said you loved me. I was just caught off-guard. I wasn't expecting it. I didn't know how to respond then, but I know how to respond now." I grabbed her by her hand. "I love you too."

She looked at me and smirked in my face. I was starting to lose my patience. Here I was, pouring my heart out to her, and she was tryna hoe me.

"So, you don't have anything to say, Sheree?"

"What do you want me to say, Rakeem?"

"Stop calling me Rakeem."

"That's your name, isn't it? You aren't lying about that too, are you? How would your *wife* feel if she knew you were telling another woman you loved her?"

Damn, she knew, but I couldn't let her see me sweat, so I gave it to her like she'd given it to me.

"I guess the same way your boyfriend would feel if he knew you'd told me you loved me."

"Yeah, okay."

She tried to walk past me to go out the door, but I blocked her.

"Look, I'm sorry I didn't tell you. I just didn't know how. Every time I wanted to tell you, I got cold feet."

She looked at me.

"Okay, bad choice of words. I'm so sorry. What can I do to make it up to you?"

"Divorce her."

"I can't."

"Why not?"

"Because we just got married."

"Get it annulled."

"Are you going to leave your boyfriend?"

Her looking away from me told me her answer.

"I thought not. Don't ask me to walk away from someone if you aren't willing to walk away your-damn-self."

"Well, the difference between you and me is I can just walk away, Rakeem! You can't. You'd have to get a divorce in order to be done!"

"I know this! But you were the one who *told* me to marry her! Do you not remember that? You gave me permission to marry her. Why would you say that unless you didn't care?"

"Because I didn't know I was going to fall in love with you, Rakeem! That's why!"

She was crying now. I felt bad as fuck. I should have known she didn't really mean it. She's a female; they never mean what they say.

"For the umpteenth time, I'm sorry, Sheree. Let me make it up to you."

"I don't think that's possible, Rakeem."

"What you tryna do to us, Sheree?"

"There can't be an *us* anymore. You're married."

"Don't say that, sweetie. You don't mean it."

I pulled her close and tried to kiss her lips. She resisted, but I pulled her closer. When she turned her head, I kissed her neck. She squirmed in my arms, but I wouldn't let go.

"I love you, sweetie. I'm so sorry. Please say you forgive me. Don't let the door close on us. I'm in love with you. I didn't realize it until it was too late. Don't do this to me. I need you."

At that moment, she stopped resisting and I went in for the kill. I had to give her a reason to continue to fuck with me. I forced my tongue down her throat, grabbing a fistful of her hair. She moaned and I rubbed her pussy through her linen capris. The amount of heat coming from her kitty let me know she wanted me just as much as I wanted her. She squirmed as I touched her spot. I unbuckled her capris with my free hand. She tried to prevent me from doing so, but it was a failed attempt. Her capris hit the floor and my fingers went to work. I pulled her panties to the side and slid my finger in her pussy just like she liked it.

I continued to slob her down as she moved her body to match the motion of my soaked finger. Her juices flowed down my hand. I felt the need to taste her. Before she could protest, she was on the sink and I was on my knees. I had her whole box in my mouth. I devoured all her juices before I went for her clit. I latched on to her clit like a newborn baby to his mother's breast. Her moans became louder. I knew she was at the point of no return and was about to cum.

I placed my thumb at the entrance of her ass. When she didn't move away, I entered. She gasped like she needed air, then her legs started to tremble. I continued to eat her while undoing my belt. She was still trembling as I freed myself from my pants and took advantage. I carefully removed my thumb from her ass and got off my knees. She was still panting as I covered her mouth with mine and entered her soaking-wet box. I wanted her to taste herself on my tongue. She tried to resist, but I wasn't going to let her. She was going to experience how good she tasted. I fucked her hard and long.

I could hear voices coming from the other side of the door, but I didn't give a fuck. It was a matter of life or death in my mind. If I allowed her to walk out that door without giving her a reason to stay, I might have never seen her again. I had to do whatever it took to make her stay. I hoped it was working. Her body was telling me it was working, but I needed her heart and mind to follow. I had a pretty good idea where her heart was, but her mind was tricky.

She dug her nails in my back. Although that shit hurt, it turned me on more. I started to pound the hell out of her. When it got too intense, I pulled out and pulled her off the sink. I turned her around so she could see her face in the mirror. I grabbed her gently by her throat and kissed her neck.

"Tell me you love me."

"Nooooo!"

I forced every inch of me into her pussy at one time and she squealed. She was trying to force me to move in and out of her, but I didn't bulge. I used all my weight to stay inside her. I felt her juices on my dick, so I knew it was working. I grabbed her by her hair and we stared at each other in the mirror. I hadn't realized I had tears in my eyes. I needed her to say she loved me. I felt like I was losing her. In that moment, she saw the desperation in my eyes. She opened her mouth to say something, but it didn't come out fast enough. In my mind, she wasn't going to say what I wanted to hear. I started pounding her from the back. Her screams became louder and I muffled them by putting my hand over her mouth.

"Do you love me?" I asked her.

She nodded yes.

"Are you in love with me?"

She nodded yes again.

"Well, say it!"

It sounded like she said I love you, but my hand was still over her mouth. I removed it.

"I can't hear you!"

"I love you, Rakeem!"

"That's not my name! What name do you call me when I'm hitting my pussy?"

I was more forceful. I pushed her down by her shoulder. She arched her back and it put her ass in a better pounding position.

"Keem!"

"I don't ever want to hear you call me Rakeem again. Do you understand me?"

"Yes!"

"Are you in love with me?"

"Yes!"

"Say it, Sheree. Tell me you're in love with me. I'm not going to stop until you do. I need to hear you say it. I need you to tell me we aren't over and that you still love me. I need you to tell me we're in this together and there is an us!"

"I love you, Keemie. I'm in love with you! I want to be with you. There will always be an us. I love yooouuu!"

My body finally gave in. It heard what it had wanted to hear. All the anxiety, fear, and desperation I'd felt left my body and entered Sheree. I felt relieved. I lay on her back and confided in her. I told her again how sorry I was and losing her wasn't an option. She turned around and looked me in my eyes. She gave me a long kiss and told me how much she loved me. She said I would never lose her. I believed her.

We cleaned up the best we could using feminine wipes Sheree had in her purse. She needed a few additional minutes to get herself together. When I made my exit, everyone was purposely trying to avoid looking at me—except Chuck and the lil chick I assumed he'd come with. I looked at him with a smirk and sat on the couch next to Scoot.

"Good looking out, my nigga."

I gave him dap and everyone started to laugh—except Chuck. He didn't find shit funny at all.

Ten minutes later Sheree came out the bathroom. She didn't say anything nor did she look at anyone. She walked right out the door and left. I wanted to chase after her, but I didn't want to look like a punk, especially after all that shit I'd said in the bathroom. I couldn't help wondering what was going through her mind. Had I lost her the moment she'd walked out the door? I decided to stick around for a few more minutes.

As soon as I got in the car, I called her, but got her voicemail. Suddenly, I felt sick to my stomach. Not knowing what Sheree was thinking made me sick. I'd never felt this feeling before. Being sick in love was no joke.

~ Seven ~

Sheree

I felt like a complete idiot. I should have known Keem had used Lolo and Scoot to get me over to their house. Now the joke was on me. After mistakenly telling Keem I loved him, I couldn't face him. I'd wanted to forget all about him. Then, out of nowhere, Chuck had texted me 'Congratulations'. I asked him what he was congratulating me for. He'd said on Rakeem's and my wedding. He knew damn-well I hadn't married Keem. It was his way of making sure I was aware Keem had gotten married. I blocked the phone number Chuck had texted me from. I was pissed. As much as I loved Keem, I'd wanted to hate him at that moment. I knew I'd told him he should marry her, but I'd thought he had enough respect for me to let me know prior to getting married.

A few weeks had gone by since the last time Keem and I had talked. I'd been avoiding him after telling him I loved him. I'd tried to keep busy with work or the kids to keep my mind off him. I'd spent more time with Menard to fill the void of not having Keem in my life. It had just made me miss him more. Sleepless nights followed. He had been constantly on my mind. We'd created so many memories in a short time span that everything reminded me of him. Slow songs on the radio. Shows we'd watched together. Food we'd eaten. Drinks we'd loved to drink. The smell of his cologne.

One time Menard and I had been riding in the car, and Carl Thomas' song *I Wish* came on. Menard loved this song, and so did I—before meeting Keem. When he turned the volume up to the max, I'd looked out the window and imagined Keem and me. Before I knew it, a tear had fallen down my right cheek. Thankfully, Menard hadn't noticed. I'd wiped it away and blamed it on the sun being in my eye. He'd continued to sing as I sat quietly, praying the song would end. As soon as we arrived home, I'd made a beeline to the shower. I let the sound of the water muffle my cries as I washed the excruciating pain I felt down the drain.

When Chuck informed me Keem had married Brittany, all the pain I'd felt turned into hate. I'd wanted to call him and confront him, but pride had immobilized me from doing so. If he hadn't had the common courtesy of informing me he was married or getting married, why the fuck should I give the pleasure of having a conversation? Fuck him! That had worked… until last night.

My phone had rung. It was Lolo.

"Hey, She! What do you have up today?"

"Nothing much. Menard took the kids out for a bite to eat. I didn't feel like going. What's up?"

"You didn't feel like eating? Girl, come over and let me take your temperature. What's wrong with you?" She laughed.

I didn't find shit funny, especially knowing she'd known Keem was married and hadn't bothered to inform me.

"Nothing that can't be fixed. Anyway, what's up?" I asked, trying to rush her off the phone.

"The car broke down. I was wondering if you could take me to run a couple of errands. I have gas money."

"When are you trying to go? Today?"

"If you can."

"Give me an hour."

"Oh... okay..." There was hesitation in her voice.

"What's wrong? You aren't ready?"

"I will be when you get here. I didn't expect you to be available this soon. I'll get dressed now."

"Okay; see you in an hour. Bye."

When I made it to Lolo's house, I'd noticed a few cars out front; one of them was Chuck's. I wondered why she hadn't asked one of the people parked at her house to take her to the store. Although I hadn't reached out to Keem, I'd still planned to stay loyal to him by not speaking to Chuck.

It was unusually warm for a fall day. I had on linen capris with a matching white tank top and duster. I'd tied the back in a knot so it would fit tight and expose my pierced belly button. My crossbody purse hung close to my hip. I hated walking into anyone's house emptyhanded, so I'd picked up a bottle of my favorite Cupcake Wine for me and Lolo.

I'd spoken to a couple of Scoot's friends on the way inside. They were saying something to me, but I'd acted as if I hadn't heard them and proceeded inside the house. Chuck was sitting on the couch next to a slim chick

I assumed was his girlfriend. I'd said a general hello to everyone and asked Scoot where Lolo was. He stated she was in the bathroom. I hollered to let her know I was there and went to the kitchen to retrieve a couple of wine glasses. I despised sipping wine out of a regular paper or plastic cup. As I rinsed the glasses in the sink, Chuck came up behind me.

"What's up?"

"Shit."

"Oh, you scared to talk to me? You let another nigga tell you who to speak to?"

"I don't need another nigga to tell me anything, but you should be thanking his ass because he saved you from going back to jail. I saw it going sideways, and obviously, so did he."

"Yeah, okay." He turned to leave, then turned back around. "You know that isn't a good look, right?"

"What isn't a good look, Chuck?"

"Having sex with a married man. I thought you were better than that." He shook his head.

"Maybe not, but you know what else isn't a good look, Chuck?" I walked so close to him that I was able to smell the liquor on his breath.

"What?"

"You hating and dry-snitching on married niggas. You know what they say, snitches get stitches. You're just mad because you will never hit this pussy again. Mad because

Rakeem took your spot and punked your ass. You aren't supposed to be even talking to my ass right now. I wonder what Rakeem would say to you if I called him and told him you were harassing me?"

When he didn't answer, I'd continued taunting him. I was going to make his ass wish he'd never told me Rakeem was married.

"I would advise you to leave me the fuck alone and go attend to that beatdown, bottom-bitch on that raggedy-ass couch. Let me worry about who I'm fucking. You're just mad it ain't you."

If looks could kill, I would've been dead as a doorknob. The veins by his temples were pulsating and his eye was twitching. I'd known he wanted to say something, but he knew there would be consequences behind it. Chuck was a bully; he didn't want any smoke. He'd turned and walked away.

I'd opened the bottle and poured half a glass. I drank it straight down and poured another glass. Lolo walked into the kitchen and tried to give me a hug. I pulled away from her and stared her down.

"What?!" she asked.

"Bitch, you know what! Why you didn't tell me Rakeem got married?"

"Because it wasn't my business to tell. Who told you?"

"Chuck!"

"Damn! Keem wanted to be the one to tell you. Have you not talked to him?"

"No."

"Why not?"

"It's complicated."

"Complicated? What's so complicated? Has he called?

"Yes, he's called, but I haven't talked to him."

"Well, that's probably why you didn't know he got married! He was probably trying to tell you."

"Whatever. Why didn't you tell me?"

"Scoot made me promise, but hell, I could've if he was going to tell Chuck. Telling Chuck was like telling TMZ."

"Yeah." I shook my head. "I'm so glad I stopped fucking with Keem."

"Wait, what? When?"

"A few weeks ago, and this is confirmation that we needed to go our separate ways."

"Girl, bye! You love that nigga. You can't stop loving someone just like that."

"Maybe not, but out of sight, out of mind."

Lolo and I had made more small talk as we drank the remainder of wine. She vented to me about Scoot's inability to keep a job. The only thing he seemed to be good at was entertaining fuck-boys. I was glad to talk about something other than Keem. I was more so hurt than pissed. I couldn't believe he'd jumped the broom and hadn't told me. I didn't care if he hadn't been able to get me on the phone. The fact of the matter was he was married when I'd confessed my love to him. That was unforgiveable.

I'd heard the front door open. There was conversation, but I couldn't quite make out the voices. Lolo was sitting at the entrance to the kitchen, so she was able to see who'd walked in. She motioned for me to get up while she was still talking shit. She made a joke about one of Scoot's broke-ass friends and we both burst out laughing. We were walking toward the living room and I was laughing so hard I thought I would pee on myself. Then I'd seen Keem. Everything got quiet. Time stood still.

Keem asked if we could talk. I'd wanted to say no, but a part of me felt I was due an explanation. Everyone seemed to sense the tension between us, probably because they knew he was married and I wasn't the bride. I felt so stupid, but I'd allowed him to follow me into the bathroom. Once we were in the bathroom, Keem had tried to persuade me to understand the reason why he hadn't informed me he had gotten married. I wasn't in the mood to hear the bullshit. He'd made his choice and now it was time to make mine. I was putting an end to this emotional rollercoaster. I was done with the slow rise to the top, only to be let down fast, with a few twists and turns along the way.

We'd entered the bathroom and Keem had tried to talk to me. When I informed him I knew he had gotten married, he'd looked desperate. He tried to turn the tables on me by saying I'd given him permission to marry Brittany. I didn't buy that shit because he still could have told me. He also tried to throw Menard up in my face. That didn't work either because Menard and I weren't married. What did work was getting me in a confined, small area. I'd had no way to run. He took advantage of us being locked in the bathroom and overpowered me. Unfortunately, he knew my body like no other man. Over a short period of time, he knew exactly what to do to make my body cream. All it had taken was one moment of weakness. He'd noticed and gone in for the kill.

He'd kissed and apologized to me repeatedly. I didn't remember my capris being unfastened. I just felt his finger entering my wet box. Juices were flowing down my inner thighs and I felt my body starting to erupt. Then he went down on me and put his finger in my ass. I had never experienced that. It had caught me off-guard. It wasn't quite a feeling of pain, but pressure that quickly turned into pleasure. I was in heaven and he sensed it. He'd taken advantage of the situation again and dove into my pussy like a diver plunging into the deep end of a swimming pool at the Summer Olympics.

He was saying something, but I wasn't trying to hear it. I was trying to focus on having an orgasm. My responses must not have been satisfactory because he'd started pounding into me hard. He'd turned me around to face myself in the mirror. It was then that I realized what he was asking me. Tears were rolling down his cheeks. He wanted me to tell him I was in love with him and I would give him a second chance. His appearance staring back at me softened me. I didn't want to see him cry. I didn't want to hurt him. I didn't want to lose him either.

I'd told him what he wanted to hear, not because he wanted to hear it, but because I meant it. Keem must have been satisfied with my response. His body went limp on my back and he'd released all his frustrations inside me. He whispered how much he loved me. I told him I loved him as well.

We agreed he'd walk out first. There was complete silence when Rakeem opened the door to leave. No one said a word. I heard Rakeem tell Scoot, "Good looking out," and everybody started laughing. I felt like they were laughing at me! I sat on the toilet and cried. I couldn't believe I had been so weak! I was in love with a married man while living with my boyfriend. Now everyone was laughing at me. This was fucked-up on so many levels. I couldn't go along with this. I had to put all this behind me. There was no way I could continue to mess with Keem now that he was married.

I'd gathered my items, cleaned up the best I could, and looked at myself in the mirror. I had to prepare myself to walk away. I took a deep breath as I grabbed the knob of the door. It was time to take the walk of shame. When I opened the bathroom door, my mission had been to locate the front door and walk right out of it. Don't pass go. Don't collect two hundred dollars. The front door was in my tunnel vision. It was locked in.

I'd held my breath and started to walk. I didn't see or hear anyone. I didn't breathe again until I was inside my car. I turned on the ignition, blasted the radio, and drove away. I looked back at the house in the rearview. I knew it would be the last time I stepped foot inside. I was hoping Rakeem appeared on the porch in a failed attempt to stop me from leaving, but he didn't. Another confirmation that I needed to leave him in the past and concentrate on my future.

The Present

~ Eight ~

Courtney

    I never have been so humiliated in all my life. Who the fuck was that woman who'd had the audacity to interrupt the biggest day of my life? More importantly, why was Rakeem sweating bullets? He looked like he'd seen a ghost. I wasn't sure if he'd heard the words of the pastor. I'd had to pinch him to get his attention. Had I not, I'm not sure he would've responded at all. Then he had the nerve to pinch me back, like I was wrong.

    I hadn't spent all this money on this wedding to be stood up at the altar. Desperate times called for desperate measures, so I fainted. Ain't no way in the world I was going to give this mystery bitch the pleasure of ruining my wedding day. I would do it first before I allowed it to happen by someone else. Thanks to my outstanding performance, I was surrounded by an abundance of people. Some were fanning me, while others were whispering to others. I still had my eyes closed, but I heard the comments being said.

    "Is she okay?"

    "Is she breathing?"

    "Who was the girl in the white dress?"

    "She was gorgeous!"

    "I bet she was an ex of that fiancé of hers."

    "It looks like she came to claim him back."

"Where is *he* anyway? He didn't bother to come check on his soon-to be-wife? So tacky!"

"Umm hmm... I bet he ran after that girl."

That last comment *woke* an already wide-awake me up from my fake faint... But I stayed in character, the theatrics I had to go through to shield myself from public embarrassment.

"Where am I?" I ask, looking around the room.

"You're here at the church, honey, on your wedding day. You fainted!" says my mother.

"I fainted?! Why? How?"

"A young lady started walking down the aisle toward the pulpit. When you and Rakeem turned to look at her, you fainted. Do you remember that?"

I lie. "No, I don't remember that."

My mother orders everyone to leave the room. Once everybody has left the room, she resumes our conversation.

"Well, Rakeem remembers, I'm sure of it. No one has seen him since you fainted. When we rushed you to the back and you started to stir a little, he said he'd be back. Are you sure you don't know who that woman is? She looked like she was about to ruin your wedding."

"Never! I would never let anyone ruin my wedding. Find Rakeem! We're getting married today!"

"Courtney, the pastor is gone. He had another engagement he had to attend. Let's just postpone the wedding until you're feeling better."

"I WILL NOT CANCEL MY FUCKIN' WEDDING!"

"WATCH YOUR MOUTH IN THIS CHURCH! No one is asking you to cancel your wedding. I'm just telling you to postpone it until you figure out what's going on with Rakeem."

"Rakeem and I are going to be fine. That female is no one."

"Yeah, okay if you say so, but it didn't look like she was *no one* to Rakeem."

I roll my eyes at my mother. Where the hell is Rakeem? I start to feel a little weird and I feel a pain in head. Then many voices that I can't make out are all talking at once. I have to grab my temples and shake my head in order to gain control. My mom notices.

"Courtney, when was the last time you took your medication?"

~ Nine ~

Rakeem

Courtney is on the floor of the church with a group of people around her. I allow them to baby her. I notice her eyes open slightly, but she quickly closes them when we make contact. On that note, I beeline out the church in search of Sheree. When Courtney *"fainted"*, Sheree turned around and walked out the church without a care in the world. I didn't want to cause a scene. People are already outside the church gossiping and whispering about today's shenanigans.

I see Sheree jump in the driver's seat of a brand-new white Range Rover. I can see life has been good to her. It has been two years since we've seen each other, the longest separation since our first encounter. I reach in my tuxedo pants pocket for my car keys, but they aren't there. They are in the office the groomsmen had converted to a changing room. I notice my boy Rod getting out of his car. It is obvious he is late. Had the wedding gone off without a hitch, he would have missed it. He is walking toward me as I am running toward him.

"What up, Rakeem?! Sorry I'm late. Traffic was a ma'fucka."

"Let me see your keys, Rod!"

"What?!"

"Give me your damn keys!"

"Okay, man. Here." He hands me the keys to his two-door Lexus coupe.

I zoom out the church parking lot. Sheree isn't far enough ahead where I can't catch up with her, and I catch up with her at the red light. Her windows are up and she's bobbing her head to an upbeat tune, ideal for someone who has singlehandedly ruined a wedding. I honk my horn to get her attention. The music must be loud. I lower the passenger window, wave my hand and honk the horn simultaneously. It works. I catch her attention and she lowers her window.

"Hey, Rakeem! What's up?"

I know this woman is crazy. She's acting like nothing has happened.

"Pull that fucking truck over!"

"For what, Rakeem? Don't you have some place you need to be?"

"Sheree! Pull the damn truck over now!"

Sheree speeds off. I pull behind her, ready to chase her down if I have to. She puts on her blinker and pulls into Olive Garden. She gets out the car and casually walks into the restaurant. The hostess asks her how many are in her party. She turns to look at me for confirmation that I'll be joining her. I neither confirm nor deny. It should be obvious, considering I'm standing behind her. She turns back to the hostess and informs her it is a party of two.

As the hostess walks us to our seats, I can't help noticing how round Sheree's ass is. Looks like she's lost a few pounds in the stomach and gained it in the ass. I sit across from Sheree and the waiter comes over to take our drink order. Sheree orders a glass of Roscato. I order cognac and coke. She looks at me and smiles.

"You look nice. How's the Mrs.?"

"Like you really give a fuck, Sheree. What type of bullshit was that?"

The waiter brings the drinks to the table. Sheree orders calamari. I guess she's planned on having a full-fledge dinner. She takes a sip of her wine and proceeds with the conversation.

"Now, where were we? What were you saying, Rakeem?"

"I was saying, that shit you pulled at the church was some complete BULLSHIT!"

"What did I do? I was invited to a wedding as a plus one, so I attended. Didn't know it was *your* wedding. How *would* I have known? *You* didn't tell me." She sips more of her wine. Her tone is vitriolic as fuck.

"I don't have to tell you shit! I owe you nothing!"

"Obviously, hence the last two marriages," she says calmly.

"So that's the problem, I didn't tell you I was getting married? That's the reason you pulled up to my shit, being disrespectful? Why do you even care? You're married. I didn't come busting in your shit, objecting to your fucking marriage. Make this shit make sense!"

"You didn't have to bust in my shit. I informed you that I was getting married. You didn't have to hear it secondhand. No one else came and told you. You didn't hear about it on Facebook. No alert on Instagram. No one tweeted it. I have enough respect for you to tell you myself. You would think, over the course of the years and me constantly trying to embed it in your head, THAT YOU WOULD AT LEAST HAVE GIVEN ME A FUCKIN' HEADS UP!"

I know she is getting upset because she is getting louder. Her eyes start to water. I have to defuse the situation.

"Look, Sheree, I get it."

"No, you don't, Rakeem. If you knew better, you'd do better."

"I'm sorry."

"You sure are."

"If you're going to keep insulting me, I'm going to leave."

"No one is stopping you. I'm sure *your wife* is wondering where *her husband* is."

She takes the last sip of her wine and gestures for the waiter to bring her another. She picks up a piece of calamari and dips it in the sauce. She looks at me, then places a piece in her mouth.

"You're still here? Thought you were leaving."

I stand up to leave. I don't need this shit. "You're right. I am."

I turn to walk away. Behind my back, Sheree speaks in a low tone, "Clown."

I turn back around. She knows how to get a rise out of me.

"What did you say?"

"I called you a fuckin' clown."

"You show up to my wedding, uninvited, and you call me the clown? You got me fucked up." I laugh.

"Do I?" she asks. "When this is all over, I'm pretty sure, Courtney will be the one who's gonna have you all fucked up. I don't know which one of y'all is more desperate, you or her? But, as always, I wish you all the best."

"You're still in love with me. That's why you're doing this bullshit."

"And you're still in love with me. That's why you're doing this bullshit." She gestures toward my tuxedo.

"Whatever. You don't know what the hell you're talking about. I'm marrying Courtney because I love her."

"I don't doubt that you love her. You're just not in love with her. You're in love with me."

I say nothing. It doesn't matter if she is right or wrong at this point. She is married and I still plan on marrying Courtney.

"Sheree, all of this is irrelevant. You're married and I still plan to marry Courtney."

She shrugs her shoulders, and gestures to the waiter to bring a carry out box and the check.

"Maybe it is, but like I told you before, the only thing that's going to keep us apart permanently is death."

I feel a chill go through my body.

"You're talking really crazy. Don't let me find out you're a psycho after all these years."

"Nah. You're marrying the real psycho, buddy."

Her look is serious and I can't tell if she is playing or not.

She stands up to leave after paying the bill and leaving a tip. She walks past me as I am still trying to process what she said about Courtney.

Midway through the parking lot, she abruptly turns around to say something. I don't realize I'm walking that close behind her and she ends up in my arms. We stand face-to-face. No words need to be said. I have tried to stay away from her when I'm in a relationship. One encounter with her and being faithful goes out the window. Today is no exception. I kiss her lips. They are still as soft as I remembered. Once I start, I can't stop. It is like a mosquito bite that needs to be scratched, even though scratching it only irritates it to the point that you have to scratch it again and again.

~ Ten ~

Sheree

Here we go again. Just like teenagers, we are in the parking lot making out. Unfortunately, we are like a moth to a flame. Not sure who is which, but we attract each other. Despite being hurt, I allow Keem to caress and kiss me. His touch always soothes me. My panties start to get wet. He must have sensed this because he reaches under my dress and starts to finger my pussy.

I brace myself by leaning on the rear passenger door of my truck. I find the handle and begin to tug on it. When this doesn't work, I reach in my clutch to retrieve my keys and pop the lock. Once I hear the door unlock, I open it with my free hand. I scoot onto the back seat, freeing myself from his touch. He looks at me as if he is contemplating whether to come inside. I notice his hesitation and begin to remove my dress, exposing my breasts. Seeing my voluptuous breasts spilling out on top of the dress gives him all the confirmation he needs. He climbs into the back seat and closes the door.

It is time to take back control. I don't allow him to put those magical lips on my love box. I unbuckle his pants and allow him room to scoot out of them as I continue to kiss him. I straddle him and we exhale at the same time, like two synchronized swimmers coming up for air after completing a vigorous routine. We are finally able to breathe again. I grind on him slowly and very strategically. I want to feel every inch of him inside me. I know I am wrong, being married and all, but I don't care. Keem will always be mine, no matter who he or I am attached to. We might "break up" periodically, but we always find our way back together.

I grab his hands from my ass and hold them up behind his head. Nothing is said. I breathe in his air and vice versa. Our heartbeats are in-sync and rapid. I lick his now-salty neck and kiss his earlobe.

"I still love you so much, Keem."

Drinking the wine so fast has me tipsy and in my feelings. I start to spill my guts between kisses.

"I still love you too, She."

"I'm still in love with you, Keem."

"I'm still in love with you, She."

That is all that needs to be said. We both know what we are doing is wrong, especially me. Keem, technically, is still single. I am not. I am a married woman in love with someone else. Someone I probably never will have to myself. Someone who is also in love with me. However, we are never in love and single at the same time.

Keem cups my ass cheeks with his hands in a failed attempt to control my groove. I stop grinding on him and kiss his neck. I start contracting my pussy muscles so it grips his dick. I feel his dick pulsating inside my vagina. I start to grind on him a little faster. I remove his hands from my ass and place them on my breasts, gesturing for him to squeeze them. He follows instructions well. He even puts them in his mouth and starts to suck them.

I start to grind faster and harder. I apply pressure to his neck as I kiss him. I am ready to explode. My head is now hitting the ceiling as I continue to ride *my* dick. He grabs my hips and we both moan on impact from the force. He grabs a fistful of my hair and puts his tongue down my throat. I take ownership of his tongue and begin to suck on it. He squeezes my nipple. It hurts but feels so good.

"I'm about to cum, Keem!"

"No, you aren't, not until I tell you to."

He lifts me up off his dick and turns me around so I am no longer facing him. I am now in a doggy-style position. He places his hand on my upper shoulder, giving me a push downward. My head is down, but my ass is in the air. He rams his dick in me all at once and I gasp loudly. I don't know if I gasped because of the pleasure, the pain, or the shock! Thank God for leather seats because I have just soaked them. He doesn't move in or out of me. He applies more pressure, pushing me further into the seat and his dick further into my stomach. He moves in a circular motion. He pulls back very slowly, relieving some of the pressure and allowing me to breathe freely. He moves in and out of me slowing. Slow motion. The anticipation is everything.

The noises our bodies make due to the wetness is a perfect symphony. I feel several beads of sweat fall on the small of my back. He speeds up a little as he lifts me back to the standard doggy-style position. He starts pounding me from the back hard. His hand is around my neck and I am sitting on his dick. He braces himself on the back of the driver's seat. He forces me up and down on his dick as he grips my neck tighter.

"Whose pussy is this, Sheree?"

"Yours, baby!

"Are you forever mine?"

"Yes, daddy!"

"Because I'm forever yours."

"Promise?"

"I promise, She. The only thing that will separate us is..."

"Death!" we say in unison.

No more words are needed. This is our bodies' cue to release and let go. We become one at that moment once again. We lie in each other's arms, neither one of us in a rush to leave, but we are in the parking lot of a restaurant. Shortly, workers will be walking out when the restaurant shuts down.

Keem is in deep thought. I'm sure he's thinking about a lie to tell Courtney. I feel guilty, but not guilty enough to tell Menard. I'm uncertain that guilt will stop me from doing it again. I have no idea where Keem and I are going from here, but I do know I'm not going to allow Courtney to have him to herself. In my mind, I'm allowing her to borrow him, not have him. I know I'm playing a dangerous game, but I don't care. I am in love with this man. Nothing but death is going to keep me from having him, and like Frank's Red Hot Sauce, I put that shit on everything.

~ Eleven ~

Courtney

I have called Rakeem's phone several times and it continues to go to voicemail. According to one of the guests, he was last seen speeding out the church parking lot in pursuit of a white Range Rover. I can only guess it belonged to the mystery woman who destroyed my wedding.

I have to listen to my mother on the ride home tell me all this could be a sign. Maybe Rakeem isn't the one for me. Maybe I should think this through before attempting to marry him again. Maybe I should focus on my mental well-being. I understand she's worried that all the stress may cause me to have a psychotic breakdown, but I got this! She doesn't understand that I have been engaged three times, married none. Each engagement had been called off by my soon-to-be husbands.

I am the only child. Raised in a two-parent household, I never had to fight for their attention with another sibling. Mommy and Daddy worked hard to make sure I had everything I needed and whatever I wanted. I stayed in designer clothes, fresh hairdos, and was the envy of my classmates. I won class best dress throughout high school. I didn't have a lot of friends. Most people hung out with me because I had my own car at sixteen; they used me for rides. I didn't mind because I used them for their friendship. Nothing more disgusting than walking the hallways of school alone every day. Loser status.

Mommy and Daddy also taught me, what happened in our house, stayed in our house. No one outside the home knew Mommy and Daddy slept in separate bedrooms. Or that they could barely stand each other. Nope, they put on a performance deserving of an Oscar every time they stepped out in public. There were rumors that Daddy *and* Mommy had outside relationships, but it was never confirmed. If Daddy paid the bills and provided a roof over his family's head, Mommy didn't give a shit. She was very superficial, so I got it honestly. Her job was to spend Daddy's money and look good doing it.

When I turned thirty, my mother asked me when was I going to give her grandchildren. I would tell her soon, but I knew early in life that I didn't want to have children. I was spoiled and didn't like to share anything. Not my time. Not my money. Not my man. Being clingy or needy was the cause of some of my relationships failing. I couldn't help that I wanted to be all in or nothing. I wanted to be my man's everything and vice versa. There was no room for anyone else. Just us. Family and friends, on occasion. But kids? NOT.

Babies would be the main topic of Mommy's and my conversations whenever we met. To stop her from asking me about babies, I told her I am infertile. It isn't a complete lie. I am infertile because I'd had my tubes tied and burned to ensure I wouldn't have any demon seeds. They say mental illness sometimes skip a generation, but I'm not about to find out.

It is now one in the morning and I am steaming. My mind is racing, and I'm rocking back and forth on the living room couch. I've called his phone every ten minutes, but it continues to go to voicemail. I conclude it is off or dead. But why? Where is he?

The doorknob turns and Rakeem walks in, looking worn out and in despair. He attempts to walk past me. I guess he thought he was going to go to bed without discussing his whereabouts. I block his path. He smells fresh, like "he'd just washed his ass" fresh.

"Where have you been. Rakeem?"

"Out."

"No shit! Where?"

"Nowhere in particular, clearing my head. Sorting some shit out."

"You couldn't bother to check on me? I fainted and you bust the hell up?"

He chuckles. "Fainted? That's what you're calling it?" He shakes his head and walks around me.

"Yes, that's what I'm calling it because that's what happened."

"Yeah, okay, sure." He continues laughing. "I'm tired. Goodnight."

He gives me a kiss on the cheek and walks up the steps. I am on his heels.

"Goodnight?! What the hell do you mean, goodnight? A bitch walked into my wedding and objects to us getting married, ruining our day for us. You disappear, then walk in and say goodnight?!" I turn him around to face me. "Who the fuck was that bitch and why did you allow her to ruin MY wedding day?"

I take notice that Rakeem's jaw tightens up when I call the mystery woman a bitch, an indication that the mystery woman means something to him.

"First off, she didn't ruin *your* wedding day; YOU DID! You're the one who faked fuckin' fainting to save face! I saw your ass! You can get over on other ma'fuckas, but not on me. I saw your ass *acting* like you'd fainted. Had your ass not fell out like a damsel in distress, you would be married by now! Just because she walked down the aisle doesn't mean she was about to object. And, even if she had objected, it didn't mean I wouldn't have gone through with the ceremony. You fucked yourself this time, boo-boo, with your dramatic ass! I'm going to sleep. Goodnight."

Feeling stupid, I ask, "So, when are we going to get married? The only reason I agreed to us living together is because we were engaged."

"I don't know. Guess we will have to talk about that. You're still engaged, but I have no problem moving out. Just give me the word."

"What am I supposed to tell everyone, Rakeem? I'm out here looking stupid-as-fuck!"

"I don't give a damn what you decide to tell them. Maybe the truth: that you faked fainting because you thought you were going to be embarrassed and stood up at the altar."

"I can't say that. What would people think of me?"

"Not my problem. But you giving a fuck about a bunch of nobodies who don't give a fuck about you speaks volumes. Goodnight."

My head starts to spin and my heart starts to race. I can't control my breathing. I rush into the bathroom and reach under the cabinet. Inside a bag I keep the trimmers I use to shave is a bottle of pills. I open the bottle with shaky hands and take two pills with a glass of water. I place the pills back in the bag and push it deep in the back of the cabinet.

I look in the mirror but don't recognize myself. I turn on the faucet and splash water on my face, taking several deep breaths. I am determined to keep it together. He had better count his lucky stars for these pills. I walk back into the bedroom to Rakeem snoring. I stand over him for a few minutes. He has no idea who he is fucking with, but he will find out if he keeps fucking with me. I guess it's time to do some investigative work. I need to find out about this mystery woman… and fast.

~ Twelve ~

Rakeem

Yesterday was the day from hell. Spending thousands of dollars on a wedding I didn't have is some bullshit. As mad as I am, I can't help thinking it is a message from God. Is He telling me not to go through with the wedding? I may have been pressured to walk down the aisle with her, but I was present and accounted for. This is the farthest she's gotten with any man in the past. I'm starting to see why.

Last night, I pretended to be asleep to avoid another argument about where I had been. She stood over me for a few minutes, as if she was contemplating her next move. I'm sure me returning home smelling like I'd stepped out the shower had something to do with that. When I returned the car to Rod, I'd taken a quick shower at his place. I would rather go home smelling like soap than another woman, especially on the day I was summoned to be married.

An eerie feeling had come over me when she finally decided to stop hovering over me and get in the bed. I remembered the sarcastic remarks Sheree had made during our conversation. She had said, when it was all said and done, Courtney was going to have me all fucked up and that I was marrying a psycho. Was crashing my wedding She's way of warning me not to marry Courtney? Was there something She was aware of that she wasn't telling me? If that was the case, why hadn't she come straight out and told me what she knows? Maybe she doesn't think I would believe her. Truthfully, I probably wouldn't have. I would've thought it was a ploy to stop me from marrying Courtney because she can't have me and doesn't want anyone else to have me either.

I was unable to go to sleep. Courtney standing over me like some crazed lunatic and Sheree popping up had my mind all over the place. I lay in the bed and contemplated my next move. I was determined to find out what Sheree meant by the comments she'd made about Courtney. I know Courtney is going to go full speed trying to make this wedding happen sooner than later, but I'm not doing anything until I'm certain Courtney is sane minded.

In fact, Courtney's sanity is only part of the reason I'm adamant about delaying the wedding. Sheree's returning complicates things again. Although she is married, I know there's still something special between us. We may not be able to pursue it to the fullest, but I must see where her head is. She was so quick to fuck up my shit, let's see how she feels when I start interrupting her happy little home. I'm no bitch-nigga, and I would never knowingly put her life in danger, or run back to her husband and tell him about us. But I can make sure I tattoo my name on that pussy every chance I get. She has me all the way fucked up if she thinks she's going to fuck up my shit and live her happy life. It is game time. Let's see who's standing at the end.

I wake up to the smell of bacon, eggs, and pancakes. Upon entering the bathroom connected to the bedroom, I hit my knee on the open cabinet. Again.

"Fuck! Why is it so hard for her to close this damn cabinet door?" I yell.

It seems like I hit my knee on this door at least once a week. Every time I ask her why she leaves it open, she has no recollection she was in the cabinet to begin with. Maybe the door is loose or off-level. I will get to it eventually, but for now, I'm ready to get my day started. Today is Sunday. I should be in marital bliss right now. We are scheduled to leave for Jamaica Monday morning. However, I'm not sure how this is going to play out. Thankfully, I informed her to get insurance on the trip. I'm not in the mood to be around Courtney for five days, especially after yesterday's turn of events.

I brush my teeth, wash my ass, and moisturize my face. The weatherman predicted it will be cool in the D today, so I opt for a Polo jogging suit and all-white Air Force Ones. I walk into the kitchen to see Courtney standing with a smile on her face, holding two plates in her hands. I look at her, at the food, then back at her. She notices.

"Hey, babe! You hungry?" she asks.

"Good morning. Not really." I stare at her.

"Well, try to eat something. Yesterday was very exhausting. Time to regroup."

She sits a plate in front of me and a plate on her side of the table before sitting down. I look at the plate, unsure if it is laced with something that will kill me: rat poisoning, cyanide, or glass. I have to think fast. After she takes a bite of food, I am convinced *her* food is safe.

"Courtney, it's a little chilly in here. Could you grab my robe from the bedroom?"

"Sure, babe!"

She pushes her chair from the table and vanishes to the bedroom to retrieve my robe. I switch my plate with hers. I have a mouthful of bacon when she returns.

"Here you go, babe."

"Thanks."

"What's on the agenda today?"

"I'm about to head out and do some tailgating with the fellas."

"Oh, I thought you and I could hang out. This is supposed to be our wedding weekend."

I give her a look to shut her down. "Yes, it is, but you clearly messed that up."

"Well, I wasn't the only person who played a part in that. Your little girlfriend showing up played a big part in that."

"She's not my *little girlfriend*. And, no, she didn't. You gave her the power when you decided to get your Jada Pickett-Smith on and put on a performance in the middle of the church. The only person to blame for *you* not being married yesterday is *you*, Halle Berry."

"Whatever, Rakeem. If you kept your little hoes in check, I wouldn't have to get my Jada Pickett-Smith on.

I wasn't going to allow her to embarrass me in front of our friends, family, and colleagues."

"But yet you ended up embarrassing yourself! She walked out of there without a care in the world. You, on the other hand, are still not married. So, who really won? Not you, that's for sure. I wasted a shitload of money on a day that didn't happen. I must answer questions from my family and get clowned on by my guys. That little stunt you pulled yesterday affected everyone, not just you! Had you just ignored her ass, we could've been married. We could've addressed that situation after the festivities ended. But you don't think." I take my finger and poke the side of my head. "You just react."

"I had to react fast, so no, I didn't think. But I wouldn't have had to do any of that if she hadn't shown up in the first place. Who invited her? And where did you run off to afterward? Did you run after her? You don't think I noticed that you came in here smelling like you'd jumped fresh out the shower last night?"

When I continue to eat and don't respond, she continues ranting. "Yeah, I bet your ass did meet up with her and fuck her with your trifling ass."

I chuckle and point a forkful of eggs at her. "You're worried about the wrong shit. Worry about why your black ass is sitting there with an engagement ring on instead of a wedding ring. Worry about getting my money back from that honeymoon that isn't going to happen because there was never a wedding. Worry about that extravagant, outlandish lie you're going to tell your friends, family, and colleagues. Worry about all that shit, not the next ma'fucka!"

I don't think she heard anything I said. She just wants to know the name of the person who crashed her wedding.

"What do you want her name for? Seems like you have bigger fish to fry to me than the name of the person you allowed to *fuck up your big day*."

"I want to know the name of the person who ruined my muthafuckin wedding day, Rakeem!"

She slams both hands on the table and stands up. She has fire in her eyes and steam coming from the horns on her head. I look up at her unphased. I dab the corners of my mouth with my napkin before placing it on the plate. I push my chair back from the table.

"Her name is Courtney."

"You have the audacity to be fucking with a bitch with the same name as me? You're trifling as hell, Rakeem."

I shake my head from side to side. "No, I'm not fucking with a bitch with the same name as you. The ma'fucka who ruined your ma'fuckin wedding is standing right here in this room, and her name is Courtney. I'm out."

I grab my phone and keys, and walk out the door. Courtney stands there in disbelief with a dumb look on her face. Guess the food she prepared wasn't poisonous after all. The only thing dead is her vibe because I killed it. I head to Scoot's house, prepared for the verbal beatdown I'm about to receive. Scoot is known to have a house full of niggas, but he knows better than to clown me in front of unfamiliar folk. I call Rod on the ride over so he can meet me there. It makes better sense to have them clown me all at one time versus on separate occasions.

I stop at the store to purchase a bottle of Hennessey Black and a Red Bull. I'm not going to go all in until we've had the conversation. I know liquor can exacerbate an already fucked-up situation quick. The last thing I need is to let the fellas see me bothered over the bullshit. I know they have plenty of questions for me, and I know questions concerning my future relationship with Courtney and Sheree are going to be the headlines for about sixty minutes.

Sheree is heavy on my mind as well. I wonder what she's doing now. How will she proceed after yesterday's events? Does she plan to tell her husband? Is she planning to see me again? I figure I will find out where her head is because mine is all over the place. Besides, I still want to know what's up with those comments she made back at the restaurant. I summon Alexa to give her a call. I know her husband is probably out watching the game with his friends, so she'll be able to talk. It isn't like I really care anyway, especially after the tomfoolery she pulled. Sheree picks up on the third ring.

"Hello."

"What's up? Are you busy?"

"Not really. What's up?"

"We need to talk… in person."

"About?"

"Yesterday."

I look at my phone in disbelief. Is she playing some type of game or something? Clearly, we have a lot to talk about.

"What about yesterday?" she asks nonchalantly.

"You fuckin' up my wedding. Us fucking *after* you fucked up my wedding. And how are we going to proceed *because* you fucked up my wedding."

She chuckles. "I see you're just as dramatic as your wife... Oops! I mean your fiancée. No one fucked up your wedding but y'all. Like I said, I was invited. Your precious little fiancée seemed to get a little nervous and wanted to put on a performance. Please tell her to stick to her day job; she did a terrible job fainting."

She laughs. I guess I'm not the only person who saw through that shit.

"That's beside the point. We need to talk. Today!"

"Pump your brakes, Rakeem. I'll see what I can do. What time are you talking? And where?"

"I'm going to be at Scoot's house. You can meet me there in an hour or so."

"Nah. I don't want to meet at Scoot's house. I don't feel like the bullshit. The last time I was over there, I took the walk of shame after our escapade in their bathroom."

"Okay; where do you want to meet, Sheree?"

"We can meet at the room about eight. I should be ready for round two."

"Look, no one's tryna fuck. We can meet at the park or something. I'm not in the mood for the bullshit or fuckin' today."

She laughs again. "Rakeem, you're asking me to meet up with you, not the other way around. I don't give a shit what you're in the mood for. When I want some of *my dick*, you're going to get in the mood. I'm not in the mood to answer questions today, but I will if it satisfies your fancy. So, you're going to fuck me how I want you to fuck me because it satisfies *my* fancy. See you at eight. I'll text you the room number." Click.

I look at the phone to see if she really hung up on me. She has. I don't know who she thinks she is. The way she just talked to me is something I don't recognize. Usually, she sits back and lets me lead. Yes, in the beginning she was aggressive, but as our relationship has grown, she has learned to trust me and allow me to make decisions. Today, she is the old Sheree. I'm not sure how to deal with her, but for some strange reason, the way she talked to me woke up the "one-eyed monster". Maybe releasing a little sexual frustration isn't such a bad idea after all. She is partially the cause of it. I will fuck the shit out of her after she tells me what I want to know.

I pull up to Scoot's house to see Rod has already arrived. My phone starts to ring. It is my mother. I take a deep breath. I'm not ready to face the interrogation I know she is ready to unleash, but I answer anyway.

"Hey, Ma? What's up? I'm kind of busy right now." I have to cut the conversation off before it gets started.

"Just checking in on you after yesterday. What the hell is going on? Are you okay? Have you talked to Sheree?"

She is rambling question after question. It doesn't surprise me that she inquired about Sheree instead of Courtney. She can't stand Courtney.

"Yeah, Ma, I'm okay. Just a little tired. No, I haven't talked to Sheree," I lie. "I'm in the middle of something. Can I call you back in a little while?"

"Of course, Rakeem. I just wanted to make sure my baby was okay. Thank God for blessings in disguise."

"What are you talking about, Ma? What blessing in disguise?"

"God stopped that sham of a wedding from going down yesterday. I would rather you be a bigamist, marrying Sheree, than you marrying Courtney. I know she's crazy. I can see it in her eyes. Something is off with that girl."

"Come on, Ma! Don't start with that again."

My mother has expressed her concerns about Courtney several times in the past. She feels Courtney is hiding something, but she doesn't know what it is. Usually, I brush it off, but Courtney standing over me as I pretended to be asleep replays in my head. I start to wonder if there are any other signs I have overlooked.

"Rakeem!"

"My bad, Ma. I was thinking about something that happened the other day."

"Watch that heiffa, Rakeem. Remember, if it's your life or hers, you choose to live. If anything ever happened to you at the hands of that bitch, I would unload the clip on her ass. You hear me?"

I laugh hysterically. My mother is tryna be gangsta.

"I hear you, Ma. I'm on top of it. Nothing is going to happen to me. But I have to go. I'll talk to you later. I love you."

"I love you to, Son. Talk to you later."

"Later, gangsta."

I hang up, still laughing at my mama, but in the back of my mind, I'm taking what she said serious as fuck. I know I have to stay two steps ahead of Courtney. From this day forward, I am on her ass like flies on shit. I turn off the ignition and walk to the door. I take a deep breath to prepare myself for what I know is to come. I don't hear a lot of noise coming from inside the house. This could be good and bad. I walk in and there aren't a lot of people to ask questions, so it will give Scoot and Rod more freedom to roast the hell out of me. Scoot and Rod are finishing up rolling a blunt. Scoot hands it to me.

"Here you go, dog. I know you're in need of this ma'fucka." He chuckles.

I grab the blunt. Scoot and Rod look at each other, in disbelief that I am about to smoke. Smoking is not something I usually do because of the random drug tests at my job. Seeing I am off for the entire week for my "honeymoon" though, I decide to take a puff or two. I'll grab some detox tea or take some pills before going back to work to make sure I'm clean, just in case.

"Pass the lighter."

Scoot passes the lighter.

"Where's your girl?" I ask, looking around the house for Lolo and the kids. I take the blunt, take a long drag, swallow, and exhale.

"She took them to a birthday party. She'll be gone for a few hours."

I nod my head as I begin to choke. The weed invades my virgin lungs and my eyes begin to water. I get up to grab a bottle of water from the refrigerator. Scoot waits for me to finish choking to death before he continues to speak.

"Man, what the fuck happened yesterday? Sheree was braver than a ma'fucka walking in that church. She was on some *Hail Mary* shit."

Scoot and Rod laugh hysterically.

"I almost shitted bricks when I saw her walk in, and it wasn't even my wedding. She came in that ma'fucka like she wasn't leaving without your ass!" They continue to laugh.

"When she stood up when the preacher asked did anyone 'object to this union', niiiigggggaaaaa... I almost pissed on myself! She stood up like the exorcist! Possessed like a ma'fucka!"

Scoot laughs with his dramatic ass. They both have tears running down their faces and are holding their stomachs. After catching his breath, he continues.

"She floated to the end of the aisle and started to float to the altar—"

"Dog! Stop saying float, ma'fucka!" Rod says between laughs.

"Whatever, dog! That girl was floating like a ma'fucka. I know I was high, but damn! When she started to float to the altar, everything went in slow motion. Rod, man, you had to be there. It was shit straight out of a movie."

He stands up and places the back of his hand to his forehead.

"When Courtney caught on to what was going on and saw Sheree standing in the middle of the aisle, she fainted like a ma'fucka, dog!"

Scoot emphasizes by hitting the floor. His reenactment of Courtney fainting is flawless. I can't help but laugh. Rod is cracking up and shaking his head at the same time.

"Damn, I can't believe I missed all that. No wonder you're hitting the blunt hard as hell."

I shake my head as he continues.

"So, what happened afterward, Ra? You grabbed my car keys and went after Sheree. When I didn't hear from you until late last night, I could only assume you ran into her. And what about Courtney? I know she had a lot to say."

"Sheree and I talked. This broad had me in Olive Garden with a hot-ass tux on. She gave zero fucks about crashing my wedding. She claimed she was invited. By whom, I don't know. Any idea, Scoot? Did Lolo invite her?"

"Not to my knowledge. I know Lolo can be messy, but she ain't that messy. She was just as surprised to see Sheree as I was. Not sure who she got the information from."

"Well, it doesn't matter anyway. What's done is done. It may have been a sign. Sheree said some things about Courtney that don't sit right with me."

"Like what?" Rod asks.

"She said Courtney was crazy and I was marrying a psycho. She kept making sarcastic remarks about it too."

"Well, crazy recognizes crazy," Scoot says.

"Sheree isn't crazy," I quickly defend her.

Scoot and Rod look at each other and burst out laughing.

"Dog! Any broad who busts up in a church full of people! A preacher! A bride and a groom! Floats down the aisle, then calmly walks—no, *floats* out the church *after* the bride faints, is psycho as fuck! She's crazy too!" Scoot says, and they laugh even harder.

The weed has me in deep thought, looking at the ceiling. I don't even respond. I'm high as hell. After minutes of laughing, Scoot and Rod notice how out of it I am. I feel Rod staring at me and I look at him.

"Nigga, what?!" I say, somewhat defensive.

Rod hits Scoot on the arm, then covers his mouth with his hand before speaking.

"Yo, Scoot! This nigga's still in love with Sheree!"

I don't respond, which eggs him on.

"This nigga fucked Sheree last night!"

Scoot, who seems out of the loop for a minute, quickly catches back on. He comes over and sits next to me. The temperature in the house seems to go up a notch or ten. I remove my Polo jacket. My irritation is starting to show.

"Scoot, why the hell you so close?! You ain't got a fan in this ma'fucka?"

"Nigga, you didn't get hot until Rod said you were still in love with Sheree. You fucked her, didn't you? How was it? Like old times?"

I can't hold back anymore.

"Fire. Like always. Like a hand to a glove." I shake my head, no longer able to deny it. "We fucked in the parking lot of the Olive Garden."

Rod explodes. "You fucked her in my whip?!"

"Nah, dog. We fucked in her truck."

"Oh, okay, because I haven't fucked in that ma'fucka yet." He laughs.

There is a long pause. Rod, being the more levelheaded of the two, speaks.

"In all seriousness, what are you going to do? Sheree is married, so the choice should be easy. Marry Courtney... right?"

"If you had asked me that question early yesterday, the answer would have been yes. But after last night, I'm not sure I should marry Courtney. Something isn't sitting right with me."

"What are you talking about, dog?" Scoot says.

"Courtney was hovering over me last night when she thought I was sleeping. It was like she was going back and forth in her head about what she wanted to do to me."

"Maybe you're paranoid. You're probably just feeling guilty because you fucked Sheree on your wedding day," Rod says.

"Not at all. I don't feel guilty about anything, especially fucking Sheree. Anyway, Courtney woke up and cooked a big-ass breakfast, as if nothing happened the night before."

"Did you eat that shit?" Scoot asks.

I nod my head. "Yes, after I switched my plate with hers."

"That's my dog." Rod gives me dap.

We change the subject and start talking about random shit. They fill me in on hood shit for the next few hours: who'd gotten locked up, who'd made it out the hood, and who'd died at the hands of the hood. We smoke, drink, and talk shit. My phone buzzes. It's Sheree. It is 7:30 p.m.

Sheree: *305*

Me: *Be there soon.*

Sheree: *K* 😊

I must've been smiling from ear-to-ear.

"What you smiling all hard for? That must have been Sheree," Rod says.

"No doubt. I got to go handle some business."

"Okay, my baby, be careful. Watch out for the crazies. Keep your head on the swivel."

"No doubt. I'll catch up with you kings later."

I walk out the door and head to my car. An uneasy feeling comes over me. Until I figure out my next move, I have to keep my head on a swivel to prevent it from getting knocked off.

~ Thirteen ~

Courtney

 I have been sitting down the street from Scoot's house for hours. What the fuck can they be talking about for this long? I'm waiting for Rakeem to come out the house. I have a feeling he is going to meet up with this mystery woman. I'm going to catch him in the act. After what seems like hours, Rakeem comes out the house. He looks in my direction and I scoot down in the seat, hoping he doesn't notice me. Why did I drive my own car? That is a stupid decision I clearly won't make again. I will surely get my mom or girlfriend's car if I ever choose to get so desperate again.

 Rakeem gets in his car and pulls off. I count to ten before doing the same. I want to make sure he doesn't suspect anyone of following him. He drives east on I-94 for twenty minutes. We are approaching the 696 freeway. Traffic is busy for this time of day. I'm having a hard time keeping up with him. Per usual, he is driving at a high rate of speed. Unexpectedly, he cuts over three lanes of traffic and gets off the freeway on Van Dyke avenue. Several cars are honking their horns out of frustration at his maneuvering tactics.

 I attempt the same stunt, but I am unsuccessful. This flock of drivers aren't as courteous as Rakeem's batch. I try putting on my blinker as well as try to force myself between the cars. They aren't having it. I know it has something to do with the fact that they are driving raggedy-ass cars. They would make out like fat rats if I hit their car, suing my insurance company and causing my rate to skyrocket. When it is clear the young male driver in the torn-down Malibu isn't letting me over, I give him the finger and hurry to the next exit. I will double-back and hit every hotel on Van Dyke. How can he be so dumb to choose a hotel on Van Dyke? That is so predictable. He's a man. They are not the smartest, which is part of the reason they always get caught. When I catch his ass, he's going to wish he'd never fucked with me.

~ Fourteen ~

Rakeem

I knew I wasn't crazy. Before I can hit the corner, Scoot calls me to tell me Courtney pulled off behind me. I guess this is the reason for the uneasiness I felt. I was usually very cautious of my surroundings. So much for keeping my head on a swivel.

I play it cool for the most part. I'm weaving in and out of traffic at a high rate of speed, which is normal. After taking Courtney completely out the way, I see an opportunity and take it. There is a small opening that allows me to change lanes and exit. Of course, it is dangerous, but desperate times call for desperate measures. I hop three lanes of traffic and exit the freeway. In my rearview mirror, I see Courtney trying to attempt the same feat, but she is unsuccessful. I do a Michigan U-turn, hop back on the freeway, and go in the opposite direction. I have eluded Courtney *this time*, but what about the next time? I have to figure something out because this isn't a game I'm trying to play.

I pull up to the hotel in search of the correct room number. It is a low-key spot I've come up on one day. I get out the car and observe my surroundings. I knock on the door several times before Sheree opens it. My mouth drops. She has on a red sheer teddy that leaves nothing to the imagination. Her nipples are standing at attention. Other than a few pieces of fabric that cover irrelevant parts of her body, the outfit is all sheer. It exposes the red tattooed heart above her swollen pussy lips.

She wraps her arms around me and gives me a long kiss. I close the door behind us as we continue our embrace. She fumbles with the belt of my pants. I try to assist her, but she swats my hand away. She pushes me against the hotel door and gets down on her knees. By this time, my pants and boxer briefs are at my ankles, giving me little room to move. She grabs my dick and looks me dead in the eyes. She sticks her tongue out and licks from the bottom of my shaft to the top. Once she get to the top, my dick disappears in her mouth and down her throat. Her suctioning abilities are almost too much to bear.

I grab the doorknob with one hand and a handful of her hair with the other. I hold her head to prevent her from moving. I'm for certain if she moves one more time, I will lose it and cum down her throat. She attempts to wiggle free, aware of what I'm trying to prevent. I regain my composure as well as control of the situation. I yank her head back, reposition my body to hover over hers slightly, and begin fucking her in the mouth. She tries to scoot backward with her hands, but loses her leverage and ends up on her ass. Because of this, I lose my footing as well, but it only puts me in a better position.

I am now on top of her as her back rests against the bed. I continue to face-fuck her. She is moaning, gagging, choking, and trying to push me off. This only turns me on more. I begin to pump harder and faster, taking the frustrations she's given me right back to her. I'm not ready to cum just yet, so I slow down the pace a little. She seems to be a little relieved because she stops trying to push me off and starts rubbing my legs. Her body and throat relax a little and her moans sound more pleasurable.

    I pull myself back enough to see her face is completely covered in her own slob. That shit takes me over the edge. The more I fuck her mouth, the more slob forms and run down her neck. The veins in my dick start to pulsate. She feels it too because she quickly takes back control. She goes deep as hell as I try to pull back. She grabs my ass and forces me back in her mouth. There is nothing more I can do to stop the evitable. I grab the back of her head and match her flow. The noises coming from her mouth are driving me crazy. I can't hold back any longer. I let go in her mouth. Determined to have control, she continues to suck me until my knees buckle.

    I fall on the side of her. She is still licking the head of my semi-hard dick when I push her off. I lie back, panting and sweating, unable to think straight. She takes advantage of the situation and sits on my face. Juices instantly run down my chin as she rocks back and forth. I'm trying to catch her rhythm so I can latch onto her clit and return the favor. Once I latch on, game over. She is trying to squirm away, but I grab her by her ass and push her closer to my mouth. She bucks faster and harder. I don't give a fuck. There is no way she's going to suck my dick the way she did and get away with it. I suck and lick as she sways on my face.

    She is panting and moaning so loud I'm sure the front desk is going to call us regarding a noise complaint. I grab her by her neck, slip one of my fingers in her mouth, and begin to suck on it. She loves to do that shit. It drives her crazy and usually over the edge. Like clockwork, her legs start to shake and she creams all over my face. My dick is back hard, so I push her onto the bed and slide on top of her. She is on her stomach, trying to catch her breath, when I lift her onto her knees and enter her from behind. She is soaking wet. I grab her by her neck and bring her mouth to mine. By this time, we are both soaking wet, a mixture of sweat and bodily fluids. I fuck her long and slow, then short and hard.

I push her head down, toot her ass in the air, and give it a hard slap. She gasps. I divide her cheeks and start grinding in that pussy slow as hell. She tries to make me go faster, but I know slow grinding makes her lose control. She is a creamer, so it is no surprise when I notice my dick is completely white. I pull my dick out, turn Sheree around by her hair, and force my dick back in her mouth so she can taste herself. Being the freak she is, she devours it and makes noises like it is the best thing she's ever tasted in her life.

I pull out and lay her on her back. I kiss her deeply as I enter her. I look deeply in her eyes as I make love to her and I notice a tear falls down her left cheek. She wraps her legs around my waist and cups my face with her hands. Our bodies are in sync. Our souls are as one. I lift her slightly off the bed by the small of her back. I am able to go a little bit deeper. She opens her mouth to say something, but no words escape her lips. I kiss her neck as she pants in my ear. She is saying something, but I can't make out the words. I'm not sure if she is whispering or whimpering.

She holds on to me tighter. I feel the dampness on my neck. I raise up to see she is crying. Not sure what type of tears they are, I kiss them all away. She brings my mouth to hers. She kisses, sucks, and bites my lips. She tells me she loves me and I will forever have her heart. I repeat the same words back to her and mean it. No one will ever hold the special place in my heart that Sheree does. No one will ever get this close again.

~ Fifteen ~

Sheree

I'm lying in Keem's arms wishing this feeling would never go away. I know I have a husband at home, but being with Keem feels so natural. Things with Menard and I are not the best; we are becoming more distant. He's spending more time in his man cave and I'm spending more time trying to avoid him. The only time we have a decent conversation is when it pertains to the kids. I feel like a slave in my home. I'm tired of being everyone's everything. Tired of being strong. Tired of being the counselor, doctor, teacher, confidant, sex slave, maid, and cook. Sometimes, I just want to be vulnerable, free, selfish, and irresponsible.

Being with Keem gives me all of that. I'm able to do what I want to do, versus what I need to do. No one depends on me for anything and I'm not obligated to give up anything. Being with him allows me to escape from day-to-day adulting. It is the piece of paradise I crave. It allows me to be carefree and happy. Keem is snoring lightly. His phone buzzes then stops. It does it several more times. Although I'm curious to see if it's his fiancée, I don't move. For as long as I have known him, his phone has been locked. I nudge him and he stirs a little.

"Keem, your phone keeps buzzing."

He reaches for his phone, presses a few numbers, and several text messages appear. I can tell they are from Courtney but can't make out what they say.

"I've got to get out of here in a minute," he says.

"I understand."

"But there is something I want to ask you."

"Go ahead."

I'm sure he can sense a change in my attitude. I don't care how married I am, him going home to another woman pisses me off.

"What did you mean when you said Courtney is going to have me fucked up when it is all said and done? You said a couple of things that day about Courtney that have me thinking. Do you know something I don't?"

"What do you mean?" I play dumb, but he catches on.

"Stop playing dumb with me, Sheree. Is there something I need to be worried about?"

"Other than she's crazy? No," I say nonchalantly.

"What do you mean, she's crazy?"

"How many other ways do you want me to say it, Rakeem! The bitch is CRAZY! LOCO! LOONEY TUNES! PSYCHO!" I circle my finger near my head for emphasis.

"That isn't telling me shit!"

"It's telling you everything, but are you listening?! You seem to be hearing only what you want to hear."

"How do you know this?"

"Have you ever looked in her eyes? That bitch LOOKS CRAZY!" I start laughing. He doesn't find shit funny.

"Is that what you're basing your assumptions off? Her eyes? I thought you were smarter than this."

"I thought you were smarter too. Obviously not, but you don't have to believe me. You will see it, trust. You will see it. You've probably already seen the signs, but you're trying to ignore them. Trust your gut and keep your eyes open, that's all I'm saying."

I notice him grabbing his things as he makes his way to the bathroom. I lie back in the bed with my hands behind my head. I know he's thinking about what I said. After a few minutes he reappears, fully dressed. He gives me a kiss.

"I have to go. Text me when you make it home."

"Okay."

That's all I can muster up to say. I'm not ready for him to leave, but know he has to go. I lie down for a few more minutes before it is time to leave. I can't tell Rakeem how I know what I know or where I got the information. I just have to believe he trusts me enough to listen and keep a watchful eye out for Crazy Courtney.

I get dressed and leave the hotel. I'm on cloud nine from the escapade Rakeem and I've just share. When I make it home, the kids have already been fed and have retired to their bedrooms. They advise me that Menard left about an hour prior to me arriving. I enter our master bedroom and the strong smell of cologne immediately enters my nostrils. The bathroom connected to our room is still foggy from recently being used. It is kind of late in the evening for Menard to be going out. I suspect he's stepping out on the marriage as well, but don't really care enough to investigate. The more he's preoccupied with something or someone else, the less I have to interact with him. I take a shower, and as I begin to moisturize with my favorite shea butter body cream, my phone begins to make a noise indicating there's a text message. It's Rakeem.

Rakeem: *Have you made it home?*

Me: *Yes.*

Rakeem: *I had a great time.*

Me: *Likewise.*

Rakeem: *But I think we need to chill.*

Me: *Oh yeah? Why is that?*

Rakeem: *Courtney is suspicious. She tried to follow me to the room.*

Me: *Wow! Sounds like a "you" problem.*

Rakeem: *Well, it may sound like a "me" problem now, but it can turn into a "us" problem if she finds out who you are. Things can get rocky in your household as well.*

Me: *Perhaps.*

Rakeem: *Act nonchalant all you want but I think it's for the best that we chill.*

Me: *Whatever. Ttyl*

Rakeem: SMH… Yeah ok. Peace.

I'm not going to let Rakeem spoil my high. I give zero fucks about Courtney following him. Am I concerned about her bringing shit to my household? A little, but it isn't anything a little leverage can't fix. If I stay two steps ahead of Courtney, I'll be okay. This means continuing to dig up more information about her that she doesn't want exposed. Medical records are normally sealed, but it just so happens I have access through someone in Personnel. I'm very strategic about the company I keep. If I can't find out something about a person, place, or thing, I know someone who can. It's time to make a few phone calls.

I know I probably won't hear from Rakeem any time soon. Courtney has him shook. Although he still has the upper hand because he managed to avoid being married, he is still in her house. He has to be a good boy and not get out of pocket. The fact that she was able to follow him lets me know he's been just a little too relaxed and careless. I open the top drawer and retrieve my pills. I take two melatonin's to help me sleep. I know I'm headed for a restless night without them. Rakeem telling me we need to take a break isn't a surprise. The surprise is how long this "break" will be this time.

Over the course of our "situationship", Rakeem has always been the one who needed to take a break from "us. It was usually when he got involved with someone new. I'd have to pull it out of him after lengthy conversations or texts. He was never man enough to tell me. Or maybe he felt that he didn't owe me an explanation. Whatever his reason for not informing me he was involved with someone else, it wasn't justifiable in my eyes.

I commend him for wanting to do the right thing in the beginning, but it's never lasted very long. Sooner or later, he would reach out and we would pick up where we'd left off. I lie back in the bed, and like clockwork, my mind starts to wander. Will this merry-go-round ever end? Will we ever be together? If so, will we be able to trust each other? Is he worth losing everything? What if I choose him and it doesn't work out? These are all the questions that invade my mental space and deprive me of getting the sleep that is needed. In my mind, all these questions need to be answered... tonight! But they can't be answered, so I lie there in limbo.

Tears run down the side of my face. I think about how much of myself I have sacrificed for my family's happiness. How I must watch the one person I love so much marry another woman again—because I fear the unknown. The fear of starting over. The fear of happiness. The fear of failure. My emotions become too much to bear. I turn over on my stomach and start to sob loudly into the pillow. My body starts to tremble as I think about losing him again. The thought alone is unbearable.

The effects of the melatonin start to kick in and the sobbing subsides. My brain goes into survival mode and anger takes over. Then hate. My revolving door of emotions has emerged. Mission "Fuck Rakeem" is in full affect. I'm going to make him choke on his words. If a break is what he wants, then a break is what he'll get.

~ Sixteen ~

Courtney

I'm not sure if Rakeem figured out I'm following him or if he just is driving erratically as usual. He crosses all three lanes of traffic and exits on the Van Dyke exit. I try to do the same, but the horns blaring from the cars and the barrier they seem to form prevent me from doing so. I can't get off until the next exit. I double-back to Van Dyke and hit all the parking lots of every hotel for five miles down. No Rakeem. Paranoia is starting to set in as I sit in the parking lot of the last hotel. Defeated and unsure of my next move, I start the engine and head home. My phone starts to ring. It is my girlfriend Toray calling. I answer, not in the mood to talk.

"Hey, Toray."

"Hey, Court. What're you doing?"

"Just finished running some errands, on my way home. What's up?"

There is no way I will volunteer information regarding my relationship to my girlfriends. As far as they know, I have the perfect relationship.

"Wanted to see if you want to meet me at Olive Garden in Warren for a bite to eat."

"I'm actually in that area already. I can do that. How long will it take you to get there? I'm only ten minutes out."

"About twenty minutes; I'm already dressed."

"Cool! I'll see you there."

"Okay! Bye!"

As soon as I get off the phone, I regret agreeing to meet her. I haven't talked to anyone but Momma since the wedding fiasco. I know she has a lot of questions to ask. I have twenty minutes to think of something, but it doesn't help to try to muster up answers when you aren't aware of the questions. I decide to make up a story instead. Get ahead and control the situation.

I take my time driving to the restaurant. I wait in the car and listen to the smooth sounds of Melanie Fiona. I'm deep in song when an attractive woman catches my eye. She is walking alone. She gives me a flirtatious smile and waves my way. I turn my head to see can she possibly be waving at someone else. There is no one else around me, so I wave back. She is sexy as hell. I'm not bisexual, but if I was, she would be the one. I'm still staring at the woman as she walks inside. My phone rings, scaring the shit out of me. It is Toray.

"Where are you?" I ask.

"Girl, a case of the bubble guts! I'm on my way now. Go have a seat at the bar. I'll be there in twenty minutes."

"UUUGH! TMI! I'll see you soon."

Tired of sitting in the car, I go inside the restaurant. I immediately see the attractive woman at the bar. The only seat available is next to her. I contemplate getting a table. She must have read my body language.

"This seat is open. Have a seat!"

"Thank you."

"You're welcome. My name is Alexis." She extends her hand for me to shake.

"Courtney."

"Nice to meet you, Courtney."

She holds onto my hand a little longer than she should. She seems to be massaging my hand with her thumb. Or am I tripping? Her hand feels a little warm. I remove my hand from hers and ask the bartender for a glass of water.

"So, what brings you out to The Garden all alone?" Alexis asks.

"Oh, I'm not alone. I'm waiting on my girlfriend."

"Okay. Your girlfriend as in your friend who is a girl, or girlfriend as in your significant other?"

"Oh no," I chuckle, "as in friend! I don't do girls."

"Really?"

I can't tell if she's asking a question or if she doubts my response. I respond to her the same way she answered.

"Really!"

"Okay; that's what's up."

The bartender appears. "What can I get you ladies?"

Alexis speaks first. "I would like a glass of Roscato Rosso Dolce."

"I would like the same."

"If we're both having the same thing, please bring us a bottle. Thank you," Alexis informs the bartender.

I interject. "No, that isn't necessary. My friend should be here any moment now. I don't want to leave you hanging with a whole bottle and the bill."

"No worries. When she comes, you can pay for the portion you drank and continue with your lunch date."

"Are you sure?"

"Yes, I'm sure. I can use the company. Man problems."

"Don't I know it," I mumble under my breath, not aware if Alexis has heard me or not.

"Excuse me?"

"I didn't say anything." Guess she didn't hear me.

"Then it's settled! Please bring the bottle. Oh, and an order of calamari and stuffed mushrooms."

The patient bartender walks away and returns quickly with a bottle and two wine glasses. He pours our glasses half full. He attempts to walk away, but Alexis gestures with her finger for him to wait. She takes the glass of wine to the head and asks him to pour another glass. She thanks him, and he walks away to put her appetizer order in the system and attend to customers at the other end of the bar.

I look at Alexis and take a sip of my wine. This is the first time I've tried it. It is delicious. I pick up the bottle and look at the label. I want to remember it for when I come back. Alexis must have read my mind.

"You can purchase a bottle to go, or buy it at Walmart."

"That's good to know."

There's a slight pause, so I decide to press the reason she took that glass of wine to the head.

"You must have a lot on your mind."

She looks at me. "Why would you say that?"

"Duuuh, the way you just downed that glass of wine." I laugh lightly. I don't want to offend her.

"Yeah, like I said, man problems. I'm from out of town."

"From where?"

"Ohio... Dayton."

I nod as she continues.

"I came to visit my boyfriend. We had an argument and he walked out on me. I don't know where we stand now."

"If you don't mind me asking, what was the argument about?"

"Him entertaining his exes. I mean, I know we aren't in the same state, but we aren't that far from each other either! Look at me! I'm not a bad-looking woman, am I?"

She pauses, obviously waiting on me to answer her question, so I do as I finish my first glass. The bartender is there to refill both of our glasses at the speed of lightning.

"No; actually, you're really beautiful."

Alexis looks at me and smiles. I'm not sure if it's the alcohol, but her features become more defined. Her eyes are beautiful and brown, with a set of naturally-thick eyelashes women out here are paying for. Her skin has a glow and is the color of honey. Her lips are full and plump. The gloss she has on is thick and silky. I must've been staring at her too long because she touches my leg. I'm brought out of my trance.

"Thank you for saying that. You're beautiful as well."

There's an awkward moment of silence. My cellphone begins to ring. It is Toray.

"Hey, girl! Are you outside? I'm sitting at the bar."

"Courtney, I'm not going to make it. Every time I get ready to leave, I rush back to the bathroom. I think I have food poisoning! I have been on and off the toilet since our last conversation. I'm so sorry."

"No need to apologize. Do you need anything? I can bring you something."

Alexis is staring a hole through me, making me slightly uncomfortable.

"No, don't worry about it. I don't think I would be able to hold it down. Next time is on me."

"I'm going to hold you to it. Call me if you need anything."

"Okay; talk to you later."

"Okay; bye."

"Everything okay?" Alexis asks.

"Looks like I've been stood up. My friend is feeling under the weather. She isn't going to make it."

"That's too bad, but now I can have you to myself a little while longer. Let's make a toast."

"Ummm… Okay; to what?"

She holds up her glass. "To new friends and relationships. Cheers!"

I hold up my glass. "New friends and new relationships," I repeat.

We clink our glasses together and proceed to drink the contents. The entire time Alexis is staring directly in my eyes. Something in the back of my mind tells me to wrap it up and go home. To make my exit. I open my mouth to tell Alexis it was nice meeting her and I'm about to go, but she speaks first.

"Looks like it's time for a refill!"

She looks at me and smiles. I smile back. What the hell am I getting myself into?

~ Seventeen ~

Rakeem

When I arrive home, Courtney is nowhere to be found. I take the time to do a little snooping. This is Courtney's house, so I have never done much digging. I just have trusted what she says to be true, but Sheree's words are hitting home. I can't rest knowing I didn't do a little homework on Courtney.

I don't know where to begin, so I head to the bedroom. I look through Courtney's separate walk-in closet and come across a big box with a lock on it. It sticks out like a sore thumb because it is buried in the back of the closet, surrounded by other shoe boxes. I grab it to see if it's heavy, but it isn't. It feels like it contains papers. There is no way I will be able to get into it and it not be obvious without having the key. I grab my phone and take a picture of both the box and the lock, then carefully place the box back in the closet exactly how I found it. I will come back to it when time permits.

Satisfied I've found something to ease my mind a little, I call it a night. I couldn't rest without having done my due diligence. If someone gives you information on a person you are about to marry, it is your duty to investigate. There are a lot of people in jacked-up relationships because they ignored the signs. I know there's a chance Sheree could be making things up to get under my skin, but there's also a chance she could be trying to tell me something.

I'm on my way to the bathroom to take a shower when my cellphone beeps. Secretly hoping it is Sheree, I make a U-turn to retrieve the message. It's Courtney. I sigh in disappointment as I read the message.

Courtney: *Do you want anything from Olive Garden?*

Me: *Yes, bring me that chicken and pasta dish I like.*

Courtney: *Ok. See you in an hour.*

Me: *Since when does carry out take an hour?*

I wait for a response, but there isn't an immediate one. I put the phone down and head to the shower. I look under the sink to grab my trimmers and body wash. My trimmers aren't where they usually are, so I go to Courtney's side. She's the only other person who could have used them. I wish she would buy her own. I don't want to see anyone's underarm or pubic hairs but my own. I'm going to have to buy her her own shit if I want her to stay out of mine.

I look under her side of the sink and come cross a makeup bag. Hoping my clippers are in them, I open it. No trimmers and nothing outside the ordinary except an empty pill bottle. I look for the label, but it has been removed. I open the bottle and sniff it, as if that will be of any service to me—it isn't. I place the bottle in the makeup bag and place it back under the sink, wondering what kind of pills had been in the bottle and why is it hidden.

I continue my search for the trimmers. They are in Courtney's drawer. I turn on the shower and the Bluetooth speaker automatically powers up. The Whispers blare through the speakers as I groom myself. I'm hungry and can't wait to eat. As The Whispers blare through the speakers, I join in like I'm the fifth member.

Have you ever been kissed from head to toe
Down your back, around to your navel
Well, you've got that coming, my sweet
I give you more tricks and treats
I'm willing and I'm able

Because I love you
Really, really love you
And I'm so damn proud of you baby

Say yes!"

I can't help but think of Sheree, wondering what she's doing. I know she's mad at me. Every time I cut her off, she turns into this cold-ass person. She goes deep down in her bones to find a reason to hate me. Each time I go back to her—and I always do—it seems like a rehab project. I break her heart, only to have to piece it back together. It isn't like I'm trying to—I want to do the right thing in my relationships—but like a drug, I always find my way back... eventually.

I get out the shower, hoping Courtney has arrived with my food. She hasn't. I check my phone to see if she's left any messages; none. It is now ten o'clock, but I refuse to blow up her phone. I make my way to the kitchen, fix a ham-and-cheese sandwich, and grab a bottle of water. I go back to the room and turn on the TV to catch the news. Still death and destruction. Our people are killing each other off at a high rate. I call the newer generation "Generation Zoo Animals" because they have no control and no regard for their lives or other people's lives. I have never seen a generation so proud to be on heroin or crack! Of course, we experimented with drugs, but it was weed or a little powder. This is a new breed. They like sniffing air fresher, drink cough syrup, and taking pills. Instead of committing crimes outside their own neighborhood, they tear up the places they live in! I will never understand it.

I turn off the news, disgusted with what is going on in my city. The sandwich does the trick and gets me off craps. Still no word from Courtney and I don't bother calling her. I turn off the light and go to sleep. I have so many things on my mind: Sheree. The box in Courtney's closet. The unlabeled empty pill bottle. All of it is becoming a lot. I close my eyes and I'm out of it in no time. I knew a deep sleep was near.

~ Eighteen ~

Courtney

I am more than a little bit tipsy. I decide to put Rakeem's order in and call it a night. Alexis appears to be more drunk than I am. When she gets up to use the bathroom, she is walking sideways. I'm surprised she makes it back to the bar. It is indeed time to leave. I'm not sure if she's able to make it home. Like I said, I'm a bit tipsy, but Alexis is on another level. Just as she sits back down, Rakeem's food arrives. I inform Alexis it is time to leave and ask if she's able to make it home.

"Does it look like I can drive? My hotel is down the street. Do you mind giving me a ride? I'll get a Lyft back to pick up my rental tomorrow," she slurs.

"Sure, I can do that."

We pay the bill and proceed to the car. I have to practically carry Alexis to the car. She is leaning on me so hard that I think we're both going to fall. We arrive at The Hampton. Alexis appears to be sleep. I call her name several times. She answers, but I can't make out what she's saying. I get out the car and walk over to the passenger door. When I open the door, Alexis vomits all over my shirt! This shit smells foul as hell and I am pissed. She apologizes repeatedly, asking if I need to wash my shirt off.

'Duuuh, bitch! What do you think?!' "Yes; I can't get back in my car like this."

"I'm really sorry. I have an extra shirt you can wear if you can get me to my room. This is so embarrassing."

"That's okay; it happens," I manage to say, but I'm steaming on the inside.

Thankfully, there is no one in the lobby. I smell and look a hot mess. Alexis appears to feel a little better. I guess so, considering the alcohol she once consumed is now on my shirt. Once Alexis opens the hotel door, I immediately run to the bathroom to remove my shirt. I clean the shirt and wipe off the vomit that has seeped through to my breasts. Considering I've never had kids, they are still perky. My bra is wet as well, so I have to remove it as well.

I ask Alexis if she can hand me the shirt through the door, but she doesn't respond. I call out several times, still no response. I cover my breasts with my hands and proceed to the bed, where she is lying down, asleep. I shake her until she wakes up. I ask her about the shirt. She stares at me but doesn't respond. I call her name again. This time she sits up slowly and responds.

"You're very beautiful."

"Thank you, Alexis. Where is the shirt? I gotta get out of here. I can bring it back tomorrow."

"Your breasts too. They look so… good."

Now she is making me very uncomfortable. "Thanks; the shirt please."

She ignores me and reaches for the hand covering my breasts.

"Why are you acting so shy? You are so beautiful."

"I'm not shy. I have to go." I try to snatch back my hand, but she has a strong grip on it.

"Relax."

She pulls me closer. Before I know it, she has her mouth on my breast. I try to pull away from her, but she has me by the waist. I place my hands on her shoulder to push away from her, but she just moves forward. Her soft lips on my breast feels so good. I call her name several times, still resisting, but she ignores me and continues to lick and suck on each breast.

When she notices I have no more fight in me, she loosens her grip, grabs one of my breasts, and begins to squeeze my nipple. She applies just enough pressure for me to experience both pleasure and pain. I moan. This must have turned her on because she becomes more aggressive. I start breathing hard. She removes her hand from my breast and places it on my leg, caressing and stroking it so smoothly that I don't realize when she starts rubbing my butt. She grips it hard and I gasp. If it weren't for my panties, juices would be flowing down my leg I am so wet.

With one breast in my mouth, she looks up at me. When we make eye contact, she bites my nipple. I moan and bite my lip. She continues to suck and lick as her other hand makes her way between my legs. I am still standing in front of her. She slips her finger inside my panties and immediately feels my wetness. She moans as she slides my panties to the side, exposing my swollen pussy lips. She uses her thumb to slowly rub my soaking-wet clit. She's barely touching it and I'm going wild. My breathing is deep and short, and my heart is racing. Seizing the moment, she enters me with her index finger, still rubbing my clit. I start to gyrate on it as she moves it in and out, faster and faster. She removes her mouth from my nipple and starts talking dirty.

"You like that, Courtney?"

"Yeeesss!"

"Tell me you like it!"

"I like iiiit!"

"Cum on my fingers, Courtney!"

As she moves her fingers faster, I gyrate on them faster.

"Cum for me, baby! Cum for me!"

I feel something erupt inside me. My legs begin to shake and I cum all over her fingers. I almost collapse from exhaustion. I haven't cum that hard in a long time. I'm about to remove myself from her finger, but she lifts one of my legs over her shoulder and buries her face in my pussy. She is slurping and licking and moaning, and I am turned back on again. I scream out in pleasure. Alexis places her finger that contains my cum in my mouth. I suck on her finger as I rock on her face.

Just as I'm about to cum, she flips me onto the bed. I'm now lying on my back with her face still buried in my pussy. She is eating it like it's her last meal. She starts doing something with her tongue that feels so good I try to back away from her. Each time, she pulls me back closer to her. She continues to devour my pussy as I moan, kick, and squirm away from her. When she sticks her finger in my ass, I lose it and scream. She pays me no attention as she handles her business by giving me the business.

My breathing becomes shallow, my legs start to shake, and a volcano erupts. Alexis licks me dry as I lay on the bed, paralyzed. She slowly makes her way to the top of the bed, looks me in my eyes, and grabs me by my throat. She puts her tongue down my throat, never losing eye contact. She kisses me so deeply that I lose myself, no longer able to distinguish whose heartbeat is whose. She removes her tongue from my mouth and kisses me on the lips. I stare at her until my eyes get heavy and I drift off to sleep.

~ Nineteen ~

Sheree

I wake up early the next morning to a beep from my cellphone. I turn over to see Menard is already gone. Truthfully, I don't know if he came home or not. The melatonin had me comatose. I open the message.

Lex: *It's done.*

Me: *Videotaped?*

Lex: *You know it! It's on the way.*

Me: *Bet!*

I wait for my phone to beep, indicating I have a new message. *Beep!* I lay back in the bed to get ready for the show. I listen to a few minutes of rambling as Lex sets up her phone while Courtney is in the bathroom. When Courtney appears, I study her body. I can't deny she has a beautiful shape, with nice perky breasts. I guess those are the perks of not having children. Lex pretends to be sleep as Courtney asks her for a shirt. When she finally *wakes up*, that's when the show starts.

As Lex begins to seduce Courtney, I'm not sure it will work. Courtney is so adamant about not giving in. Not many women—straight, gay, or bi—can resist Lex. She is the best of both worlds. She can be every man or woman's fantasy, depending on what you're craving. I met Lex through a mutual friend about five years ago and we became cool. At first, we all hung out as a group. Once we exchanged numbers, we started texting and meeting up for drinks. She never came on to me, maybe

I wasn't her type, but I wasn't offended. Everyone is not for everyone.

I am brought out my trance by the sound of moaning. When I look at the phone, I see Lex massaging Courtney's clit with her thumb while sucking on her breast. *Courtney is bucking as Lex gives her the business. When Lex starts eating Courtney, I almost lose it. She is slurping and sucking as Courtney juices run down the side of her face. Courtney is rocking back and forth. I'm not sure if she's riding Lex' face or trying to get away from her.*

It starts to turn me on. My fingers start to move down to my already-soaked spot. I play with myself as Lex pleases Courtney. I imagine Rakeem is pleasing me. When Courtney cums, so do I. Thinking it is over, I put the phone down and go to our connecting bathroom to retrieve a towel to clean myself off. I hear more moaning and run out the bathroom to see Lex is still at it, but Courtney is in a different position.

She continues to suck and lick as Courtney begs and pleads for her to stop. She tries to get away several times, but Lex' aggressive ass isn't having it. She's eating her pussy like she's an inmate on death row getting served her last meal before execution. Courtney's body starts convulsing as Lex holds her in place until she's finished. Lex is still licking as Courtney continues having aftershocks from the earthquake she has just experienced.

When she is satisfied she has licked Courtney bone dry, she moves to the top of the bed and begins kissing Courtney in her mouth. She pulls away, but Courtney seems to yearn for more. She caresses the side of Courtney's face and looks into her eyes until Courtney starts snoring. Once Lex is sure Courtney is sleep, she gets up and tiptoe over to the phone. She looks directly in the camera and flicks her tongue fast like a snake before pressing 'Stop' to end the video.

I stand up from the bed and clap my hands as if they are in the bedroom with me. "Bravo!" I say to an empty room. I am ecstatic! I pick up my phone to call Lex. She picks up on the first ring.

"Biiiisssshhhhh! You did that!"

"You like?" Lex responds.

"Bish! No, I love! You need an Emmy! You acted like you were really into it!"

"Bitch, I was. Her pussy was quite tasty! I may have to sample that again."

"The more you fuck her, the more leverage I'll have on her ass. Wait, did you get her number?"

"Is fat meat greasy? Of course, I did. While she was sleeping, I used her thumb to unlock her phone. I called my phone to get her number then deleted the call. She was buzzing so tough, she won't remember if she gave me her number or not. Why are you asking?"

"Duuuh! So you can still smash—if she allows you to, that is."

"What are you tryna say?"

"I'm saying she may decide your pussy-licking skills ain't shit and not fuck with you anymore. LOL"

"Never that. I could get your ass if I wanted to."

"Hell, I ain't gonna lie, you had me touching myself. If Courtney weren't so selfish, she could be me and Raheem's sister-wife. Lol."

"Lol! Don't forget about me! I wanna be a sister-wife too. You and Courtney, fuck yeah!"

"Whatever, girl! But for real, do you think you'll be able to go all the way with her? The whole nine?"

"What's my name?"

"The Almighty Lex!"

"That's right! So you know the answer to that question. She won't even know who Rakeem is once I'm done with her."

"Aaahhh shit! Harriet, get the strap! Lol"

"Got it! So, what're you going to do with the recording?"

"Hold on to it until you get me more!"

"Bitch, this is going to cost you!"

"Cost me what?"

"I saw a pair of Gucci boots that would look good on my pretty-ass feet."

"Send me a pic. If you deliver, then I deliver."

"Bet!"

"Okay, porn star, let me get up and get my day started."

"Lick-'em-low Lex, signing out."

"Bye! Lol."

"Peace!"

~ Twenty ~

Rakeem

It's about three in the morning when Courtney tries to sneak in the bed. I pretend to be sleep in the same manner she'd pretended to faint. I don't budge as she slides in the bed and turns her back to me. This is a first. She usually is all over me once she crawls in bed. She smells like alcohol and a fragrance I'm not familiar with. I take a mental note as I try to drift back off to sleep. I don't know what she is up to, but it furthers my suspicions. Lately, everything she does seems suspicious. I don't know if it is because of the conversation I had with Sheree or the unexplained pill bottle I found under the sink. Times like this is when I need God to send me a sign that I'm doing the right thing.

At this point, Sheree has nothing to do with it. I need to know if I'm making the right decision for me! Sheree already is established in a relationship. No matter how much she tells me she loves me, the truth of the matter is she's married. I know she isn't as happy as she should be, but she is content. From the outside looking in, it looks as if her husband really loves her. There is no doubt in my mind that Courtney loves me, but sometimes love isn't enough, and I have no time to deal with emotionally-unstable women. Don't get me wrong, I know everyone has their demons, but I choose what demons I want to deal with.

It hasn't been a week and I'm missing Sheree like crazy. I know she's still mad as hell at me, so calling or texting her probably won't do. The only thing that get us back in a good place is a good fuck. All texting is going to do is give me some dry-ass, one-word responses that will surely piss me off. I wonder if she is thinking about me like I'm thinking about her. I wonder if we can ever truly be together, happy and faithful. One can only hope. I guess time will tell.

I wake up the next morning before Courtney with a hard on. Not one to waste a good hard on, I turn over to a sleeping Courtney. She is snoring lightly with her back to me. I lift her leg so I can get between her thighs. She purrs as I begin to play with her already-wet kitty cat. In the back of my mind, I wonder what she dreamt about that has her wet already. Can she be thinking of another nigga like I have been thinking about Sheree?

My paranoid thoughts must have taken over because I ram my dick right inside Courtney's wet pussy. She is taken back by how rough I am early in the morning. She gasps and dig her nails in my thigh in a failed attempt to get me to pull out, but it only excites me. I lift her leg higher and begin to fuck the shit out of her. She is moaning loudly as she tries to break away from my grip. I grab a fistful of her hair and yank her head back.

"Where the fuck you going? You don't want this dick?"

Her mouth is open and there are sounds, but they are unintelligible. Because she failed to answer my question and she's still scooting away from me, I flip her on her stomach and continue to hammer her from the back. I push her head down into the pillow and apply more pressure to her lower back. I'm knee-deep in her pussy as she screams my name.

"Take this dick!" I slap her ass.

One thing I like about Courtney is she allows me to have her anyway I want her. She doesn't mind me experimenting in all three holes. If I'm satisfied, she's happy. But that also goes for Sheree. She's a freak as well. We can do it wherever, whenever, and however. I'm bought out my trance by the sound of Courtney's voice.

"Fuck me harder, Rakeem!"

I separate Courtney's ass cheeks with my hands and cock my leg so it's resting on her ass and begin pounding her. She's panting as I grab her lightly by her neck.

"Cum on this dick, bitch!"

"Okay, daddy!" She starts bucking wildly against my dick.

"CUM ON THIS DICK!" I yell louder as I slap her ass.

This time she does as she's told. Her legs begin to tremble, her pussy pulsates, and I feel her liquid on my thigh. I slow down the pace a little and begin to long-stroke her slowly. She starts to shake again when I speed up the pace. I'm almost there as well. Determined not to come inside her, I pull out, grab her by her hair, and force my dick in her mouth. Her head game is strong and I'm enjoying it more than I enjoyed the pussy, so much so that I decide to prolong my nut.

I control the pace by keeping my hand on her head. She slows down. My leg is wet from the obsessive saliva coming from her mouth. She's making all the right noises. I force my dick deeper down her throat. She gags but I don't let up until she pushes back, beginning to choke. I begin to fuck her mouth with my dick. She tries to put a little distance between us by scooting back to the headboard, but I'm on her. I continue to fuck her mouth as her head bangs against the headboard. I know she's wondering what's gotten into me. I'm wondering the same about her, sneaking in the house in the middle of the night. Nah, I can't let that shit fly. Since I can't beat the shit out of her physically, I'm gonna beat the shit out of her mouth, pussy, and/or ass.

She starts to gag again. This time I'm not letting up. She is gonna learn today. I grab her by her hair again and force my dick further down her throat. I pause to give her a moment to stop gagging and relax her throat muscles. Then I continue fucking her mouth for another few minutes nonstop. Her face is wet from slob. I can tell she's tired, so I give her some encouraging words to keep her going.

"Keep sucking this dick! I'm almost there."

These must have been the encouraging words that are needed because she gets her second wind and starts sucking like her life depends on it. I can't hold back any longer. I pump faster and faster in her mouth. She feels my dick get stiffer and tries to pull back like she isn't about to swallow my seed. I grab her by the back of her head as she struggles to get away. I hold her head in place as I cum in her mouth. I don't let go until I'm confident she has swallowed every drop.

I grab my phone and head to the bathroom. I bet she will think twice before bringing her ass in the house again that late. And my food had better be in the refrigerator!

~ Twenty-One ~

Courtney

I don't know what came over Rakeem this morning. I'm almost ashamed to admit I liked it. He was freaky, aggressive, and assertive. The nastier he talked, the more turned on I was. I believe I heard him call me a bitch at one point. Hell, I didn't care. He could've called me another woman's name and I would've let it slide. I feel kind of guilty for my indiscretions with Alexis last night. We didn't have sexual intercourse, but it was still cheating.

It had felt so good! Alexis was patient, gentle, and attentive. She knew my body as if she had studied it for years. I had wanted her to stop. I had tried to make her stop, but my body had had a mind of its own. It wanted what it wanted. She made my body feel soooo good! I had experimented in college, but it had been nothing to write home about. If I had never revisited the situation again, I wouldn't have cared. Alexis had made me reconsider.

'I wonder if Rakeem would be open to a threesome?' Nah, fuck that. That usually ended fucked up for the person who'd initiated the hookup. The females usually run off with each other and the man (usually the initiator) is left holding his dick, alone. I don't have a dick, but I don't want to be on the short end of the stick. If I have a threesome, it must be with a random chick, someone I plan on never seeing again.

It is a beautiful fall Sunday morning. The sun is shining, and the ground is painted with orange, red, and yellow leaves. It is a little brisk, enough for a light jacket. Perfect weather for a refreshing walk through the neighborhood. As much as I want to enjoy the great outdoors, I don't have the energy. Between my late night and early morning sexual escapades, I am worn out.

Rakeem never comes back to bed after he fucked the shit out of me. He gets in the shower, gets dressed, and leaves. I'm not sure if he heard me come in late this morning or not. I reach for my phone on the nightstand and call him to see where his head is. The phone rings several times before going to voicemail. I decide not to call again. If he is upset, I'll give him his space. If that isn't the case, he'll call back once he sees the missed call. As I'm putting my phone back on the nightstand, it beeps, indicating I have a text message.

Alexis: *Thanks for making sure I got back to my room safely. I appreciate it. How can I thank you? Dinner?*

Hell, she thanked me enough last night! I don't remember giving her my number, but it's possible. I was drunk as shit too.

Me: *No need to thank me. I would have done that for anyone.*

Alexis: *So, are you saying no to dinner?*

Me: *I'm engaged.*

Alexis: *And…*

Me: *I can't be with you like that.*

Alexis: *Be with me? What are you talking about? I just want to give your shirt back and*

>take you out for dinner and drinks to show my gratitude for what you did for me.

Is this woman crazy? Is she just going to ignore the fact that she ate my pussy like she was at a pie-eating contest? Wait! Does she remember? She was drunk as hell. Against my better judgement, I decide to entertain the thought of dinner. I also want to probe to see if she remembers the interaction, or is she one of those "drunk lesbians"? You know, the females who are only attracted or show their attraction to other females when they are intoxicated.

Me: *It isn't necessary. You don't have to do that.*

Alexis: *How about tomorrow?*

Me: *Tomorrow what?*

Alexis: *Dinner and drinks.*

Me: *Tomorrow is not a good day.*

Alexis: *I won't keep you out too late. See you tomorrow?*

She is persistent as fuck.

Me: *Okay. Tomorrow at six is good.*

Alexis: *Okay. I will send you the location. I will keep it in the same area as before if that's okay with you.*

Me: *That's cool. See you tomorrow.*

Alexis: TTYL (kissing face emoji).

I feel revived and energized, not sure if the text conversation with Alexis has anything to do with it or the multiple orgasms in a twenty-four-hour period. I jump out of bed and head for the shower. I'm going to cook Rakeem a hell of an "I apologize, but you don't what I'm apologizing for" dinner: oxtails, black-eyed peas, mac-n-cheese, collard greens with turkey tails, and cornbread. His favorite. It is already eleven o'clock, so I have to get on the ball. The oxtails alone take a few hours to cook and bake.

The stand-up shower with the multiple shower heads massages my entire body. As much as I want to indulge longer, I cut it short before I end up too relaxed. I lotion and spray my body with my favorite Bath & Body Works fragrance, A Thousand Wishes. The smell is so enticing. I decide on a nice DKNY jogging suit. I'm not in the mood for anything clingy. Although I no longer have menstrual cycles, I still have to deal with all the symptoms—the mood swings, cramps, irritability, and bloating, etc. It must be almost that time because even the necklace around my neck is a bother.

The grocery store isn't as packed as I'd thought it would be. I must have come in between the senior citizens running errands in the morning and the church folks returning home to cook dinner for their family. I'm able to get in and out in a breeze. Usually, I would be behind someone with a shitload of groceries or a senior citizen confused on how to use their debit card, but the gods were on my side today. They know I don't need any distractions or hiccups to prevent me from getting my dinner started.

I turn the music on full blast as I head home in a great mood, determined to stay that way. Despite Mom's advice, I haven't started back taking my medication. I flushed the remaining pills down the drain. If I feel an episode coming on, I will go to the pharmacy and get a refill. Jagged Edge's *Let's Get Married* is playing and I can't help thinking of my own fiasco of a wedding that almost took place.

Rakeem hasn't mentioned anything else about getting married, and I'm starting to get worried. Why isn't he pressed? Is he having second thoughts about marrying me? I have to get to the bottom of it and fast. Tonight will be the perfect time to bring it up. After a meal like this, how can he shut me down? I drive the rest of the way home in silence as I envision how the conversation is going to go. I decide to stop at the store to grab a couple of bottles of wine. I think I'm going to need it.

Once I arrive home, I waste no time in the kitchen. I clean and season the oxtails and turkey tails before putting them in their separate pots to boil. Afterward, I soak the peas, and clean the greens to add them to the turkey tails. Satisfied that most of the cooking is started, I straighten up the living room and put a load of clothes in the washer.

Rakeem still hasn't returned my call. I'm not worried. I conclude he is aware I came home late and has an attitude. Not really pressing the issue, I carry on my day without a care in the world. I turn on my Bose Bluetooth speaker and connect it to my cellphone. I need something upbeat to add a little more pep to my step. I scroll down my list of Pandora Stations until I find Ciara. Her station never disappoints. You can work out to the list of artists the station pairs together. Missy Elliot, Chris Brown, and Megan Thee Stallion will have you sweating it out or slow grinding with a broom in hand as a mic. One of my favorite tunes, *Ride* by Ciara, comes on first. This song always makes me think of riding or the reverse cowgirl position.

> I can do it big
> I can do it long
> I can do whenever or however
> You want
> I can do it up and down
> I can do circles
> To him I'm a gymnast
> This room is my circus
> I market it so good
> They can't wait 'til you try me
> I work it so good
> Man, these niggas
> Tryna buy me
> They love the way I ride it ('cause I do it good)
> They love the way I ride it ('cause it feels so good, yeah)
> They love the way I ride it ('cause I do it good)
> They love the way I ride the beat
> How I ride the beat
> I ride it, they love the way I ride it

    I pretend Rakeem is sitting on the couch as I seductively approach him. I'm trying my best to be as sexy as Ciara is in the video, but I'm failing miserably. I'm no J-Lo, but I can grind, twerk, and roll a little somethin-somethin. I try to do a little dip, followed by swinging my hair and head like a mad woman, but end up so dizzy that I stumble. Thankfully, the arm of the couch breaks my fall. I gain my composure and decide it's best if I head back to the kitchen.

Once all the food is on the burners or in the oven, I decide to take another quick shower and put on something a little sexier, but not quite lingerie. I decide on a revealing BeBe lounge short set with my cheeks hanging out the bottom. A bra isn't an option with a set of titties like these, so I let them hang freely, up high of course. No sagging tits over here.

'Think I'll send Rakeem a little nude pic before I get dressed. This should get his ass back home soon.'

I grab my phone, hold my stomach in, check my angles, and snap multiple pictures. I take the cutest one, and click 'Message'. When my most-recent contacts pop up, I click Rakeem's number along with what I think is the right contact, and hit 'Send'. I place the phone on the nightstand as I continue to get dressed.

Beep!

Alexis: Um, I don't believe this was meant for me but I will take it.

I have mistakenly sent Alexis the nude pic! She was the last person *I'd texted*. I thought I'd selected Rakeem, but he was the *last phone call* I'd placed. Fuuuccckkk!

Me: No that was not meant for you. I was trying to send it to my fiancé. My bad. Please delete and disregard.

Alexis:	No apology needed. Nice body. Your fiancé is a lucky man.
Me:	Thank you.
Alexis:	You're welcome. But I think I'm going to hold on to it. Maybe save it to my phone so every time you call or a text it pops up.
Me:	I would prefer you delete it.
Alexis:	Ok, I will. After I see you tomorrow. TTYL
Me:	SMH... TTYL

I need to be more careful. I proceed to send the picture to Rakeem. Hopefully, he has the same reaction Alexis had. After ten minutes of no response from Rakeem, I regret sending it to him. I understand he is pissed off, but he could have at least sent a smiley face. He's really trying to get under my skin, but I'm not going to allow it. I need to be in a good head space for the conversation later. If I go into the conversation aggressive and hostile, I won't get what I need out of him. The old saying, "You catch more bees with honey than shit"? True!

Food is done, table set, and it's time to relax. I call Rakeem one last time to see how long he's going to be. He answers on the third ring.

"What's up?"

"Hey, babe! What time do you think you'll be heading home?"

"Not sure; why?"

I'm silent for a minute, trying to hear background noises to get a clue as to where he might be.

"I cooked your favorite meal. Wanted to spend a little time with you."

"Is that right? You weren't trying to spend time last night."

"Today is a new day. Let's not revisit the past. What time can I expect you."

"Give me a couple of hours."

"Okay; bye."

"Bye."

'He's Lawry's salty.' I laugh out loud, shaking my head. *'Oh well, he'll get over it.'*

Rakeem makes it home a little after seven and gives me a kiss on the cheek.

"Food smells good."

I can tell he's still a little salty, but at least he acknowledged the food and gave me a kiss.

"Thank you."

"I'm going to take a shower."

"I'll have your plate ready and waiting for you."

"Bet."

I make sure Rakeem has a healthy plate of oxtails. He loved the sides, but the main attraction of the night is the oxtails. When I hear the shower turn off, I put his plate in the microwave so it is to his liking. He comes into the kitchen just as I'm replacing his plate with mine. I place his plate along with a glass of lemonade in front of him. The microwave beeps, and I retrieve my plate and sit down. We say grace and start to smash.

Rakeem eats in complete silence, apart from the occasional sounds, letting me know I have his approval. I decide to allow him to finish most of his food before asking him about the wedding. No time like the present. Here goes.

"Rakeem, have you given any thought into setting a new date for the wedding?"

"No, not really," he answers without looking up.

"Why is that?"

"Because it wasn't me who fucked up the wedding in the first place. That was all you. Maybe you didn't want to get married. So, no, I haven't given it a second thought. It is what it is."

"So, you're going to sit here and accept no accountability for the role you played? Are you forgetting your sidepiece was there, about to ruin everything?"

"She is not my sidepiece. There's a difference between *about to ruin* versus *ruining*. You see, she was *possibly about to ruin* our wedding, but you *ruined* our wedding, so I'm going to need you to accept responsibility for *your* actions."

"I can see we're not going to ever agree on this—"

"Not at all." He cuts me off.

"So, let's move forward. Do you have a preference on another date?"

"Maybe May or June."

"What?! That's about six months away!"

"And? What's the rush?"

"No rush, but why so far out? You don't want to marry me anymore?"

"Look, Courtney, it isn't that I don't want to marry you. I just want to make sure marrying you is the right thing for me to do. Lately, I have been noticing some things that have me apprehensive."

"Like what?"

"Nothing I want to talk about at the moment."

"Well, how am I supposed to change or address your concerns if you don't tell me what they are?"

"The concerns aren't for you to address or change. They're for me to observe and decide if they're something I want to live with for the rest of my life. Me telling you what they are will just prompt a temporary change in you. As soon as the dust settles, you will resort back to your old ways. Pushing the wedding out will give me and you the time we need to see if this is something we both want to do."

"Does this have anything to do with last night?"

"No, it doesn't."

"Are you going to even ask me where I was?"

"Should I have to? If you want to tell me, then tell me. If not, so be it."

"So, you don't care?"

"Obviously not as much as you want me to care." He looks up from his plate.

"I ran into an old friend at Olive Garden. She happened to be in town for the weekend visiting her boyfriend. She drank a little too much and I escorted her back to her hotel room."

"That's pretty noble of you."

"Yes, I know."

"Guess my food wasn't a priority."

"I apologize for that. I was having a good time catching up. The food is in the refrigerator."

"Okay."

"So, that's it?"

"What else you want me to say, Courtney?"

"I just want you to give a fuck more! Damn!"

He laughs. "No, you just want me to be a little more jealous."

"Well, yeah!"

"You know that isn't my style. Wait… maybe you don't know. Hence, why it's best to push this wedding out further. Obviously, you don't know me as well as you think, and vice versa."

He stands up from the table, scrapes and rinses his plate, and puts it in the dishwasher. Before heading to the bedroom, he turns to me.

"Oh, and you got me fucked up if you think I believe it took you four hours to *escort* your *friend* back to her hotel. Olive Garden closes at eleven."

I open my mouth to say something, but he cuts me off.

"No need to explain. Good night."

And he walks away.

Although I *figured* he knew, that didn't stop the gut punch I felt *knowing* he knew. Guess I've got to be more careful. I'm not a cheater, never have been. But there is something about Alexis. She makes me feel comfortable and sexy, but that no longer matters. Alexis is and will only be just a friend. Nothing more.

~ Twenty-Two ~

Sheree

Days turn into weeks and I still haven't heard from Keem. I try to say busy to keep from contacting him. So far, it has worked. Things at home between Menard and I are much better. He's staying home more as well as being more involved with the kids. Date nights are becoming more relevant as well. Sometimes we do dinner and a movie; other times, we go for walks on the Riverwalk. We are having more sex and it seems to be better than before. I don't know what his side-chicks taught him in the streets, but his skills have improved dramatically.

I can't lie, there are times when I think about Keem. Many times, I've wanted to call out his name during sex with Menard, but I bite my lip instead. Yes, I miss him dearly, but he said what he said and I'm going to try my best to abide by his wishes.

Like a usual Friday night, Menard and I are having date night. We decide to splurge on an upscale steak house, Ocean Prime. We sit down and make small talk until the waitress brings the menus and water. I look around the restaurant and nod my head.

"Nice ambience and atmosphere," I say.

"Yeah, it is. I bet the price on the menus is going to reflect such." We both laugh.

"For sure."

The waitress brings bottled water and menus to the table. She asks if we want to order drinks.

"Yes; please bring me a Lemon Drop."

"I would like Remy VSOP on the rocks, light rocks." Menard says.

He continues speaking to me, "For these prices, the food had better be the shit!"

I look at the menu and nod my head in agreement. "I know, right?! So, how was work today?"

"It was okay, meeting after meeting. I don't know why the big bosses don't understand that you can't make money if you're in meetings all the time. Most of the time, the shit can be addressed in an email."

Menard is the plant manager at a local car parts factory. He's been a loyal employee for ten years. He started on the assembly line, then became a team leader and supervisor, before becoming a manager. He continued his education at the University of Phoenix, earning his bachelor's degree in Management.

I am proud of his accomplishments. He'd worked full-time while attending school for years. This had made things harder and more stressful in the household. He was never there and I seemed to always be there. I attended to the kids before and after work. If I wasn't attending to them, I was making sure dinner was cooked, clothes were washed, and the house was clean. I never had time for me. I was giving my all to my family and losing myself while doing so. Sure, I had successfully completed college and was making decent money in a field I loved, but I still felt incomplete, unwanted, and unappreciated.

Every time Menard and I separated, it was my decision. I was tired of being responsible and depended on. Although I missed Menard at times, I'd enjoyed every other weekend the kids spent with him. It gave me the alone time I needed and craved, a sense of freedom. By the time we'd reconciled from our last separation, the kids were of age and able to do for themselves as well as complete household chores. Unfortunately, this allowed me to have more idle time on my hands. The saying, "An idle mind is the devil's workshop," is true as fuck. That's when I met my "devil" and what a handsome devil he is.

"Sheree! Sheree!"

Menard is calling my name.

"Huh?" I had been in deep thought and wasn't sure how long Menard had been calling my name.

"Are we doing appetizers?"

"Yeah, why not. You choose."

I hadn't paid much attention to the menu, so I have no idea what the choices are.

"Let's try their Point Judith Calamari."

"Sounds good to me."

The waitress comes back with our drinks and takes our appetizer order. My Lemon Drop is nice and strong. I have to refrain myself from drinking it in one gulp. I decide to order the twin lobster tails with asparagus. Menard orders the surf and turf, medium well, with garlic mash potatoes and mixed vegetables.

The food is delicious! The steak is tender and the lobster cooked to perfection. We are enjoying each other's company and we order another round of drinks. We continue to converse with each other as we eat our food. I look up from my half-eaten plate to see the host escort a couple in our direction. The woman is looking back at her date, talking to him, but you can tell he's only half listening. My eyes meet his.

Out of all the restaurants in the State of Michigan, City of Troy, THEY picked this restaurant on THIS day at THIS time! Rakeem and Courtney! I'm sure Rakeem and I both are relieved when the host stops two tables shy of where Menard and I are sitting. He directs Courtney to sit with her back to me. I purposely hold the dessert menu to my face so she never gets a look at me. If she gets a good look at me, that could have ruined everyone's night.

I down my remaining Lemon Drop, make eye contact with my waitress, and order another one. She looks at Menard to ask if he's also ready for another drink. I shake my head no because he's still nursing his first drink. I continue to eat my food in silence. I can feel Keem staring at me, but I refuse to look in his direction. Courtney is running her mouth about finalizing their wedding plans. I hear Keem ask her to give it a rest for the night and talk about something else. She lands on a conversation about redecorating their home. Menard excuses himself to use the restroom. My phone beeps.

Keem: 😊

Me: *Fuck you.*

Keem: *It's like that?*

    I decide not to respond. I smile at him, which causes him to smile a little. I give his ass the middle finger and the unbothered look that goes with the finger. His smile disappears quickly and he picks up his menu. I continue to drink my drink as I stare a hole into Keem. My intention is to make him feel as uncomfortable as I felt when he walked in. People don't understand the power of energy. Just that little interaction gives me the power back. Now he feels what I felt. Now he feels drained. Now he feels just as fucked up as I did when he told me we needed to chill. By the time Menard comes back from the restroom, I'm back to my normal self.

    "Do you want some dessert?" I ask Menard.

    "No, I'm stuffed."

    "I think I would like something."

    "Really? You usually are too full to eat dessert. You're still hungry?"

    "No, I'm full, but the dessert looks so good."

    Truthfully, I don't really want dessert; I'm just not ready to leave. I want to sit and continue to fuck with Keem a little more. I know it's risky. If she turns around and recognizes me, it could be the end of my relationship as well as his. But I don't care, not at this moment. I'm ready to risk it all just to fuck with him. Let the chips fall as they may.

I order the chocolate peanut butter pie. I'm finishing up my third drink when I see Courtney excuse herself from the table. She heads in the direction of the restrooms. I turn my head and act as if I'm retrieving something from my Tory Burch clutch. My phone beeps.

Keem:	*So is this game you want to play? You're just going to ignore me?*
Me:	*Didn't you say we needed to chill? This is me chilling. I would appreciate it if you would lose my contact information. Thanks!* 😊
Keem:	*Lol. Yeah right. That ain't what you want. You know it's not.*

I delete the message, block Keem, and put my phone on the table. I know if he continues to text me, he'll get the notification he is blocked. Just as I thought, he continues to text and sees he is blocked. I give him a smirk as I place a piece of the pie in my mouth. I lick my lips seductively as I continue to look in his direction. To add insult to injury, I put another piece of the pie on my fork and instruct Menard to taste it. I feed him several bites before eating a few more myself. Satisfied at the steam coming from Keem's head, I place the fork down and dab the corners of my mouth.

Out of the corner of my eye, I see Courtney returning from the restroom. Keem notices and adjusts his attitude as she approaches the table. When she sits down, I inform Menard to take care of the check, I have to use the restroom.

The restroom is in the back of the restaurant. The stalls are updated and the décor is immaculate. I take mental notes when I see a few little tips that can really make a bathroom look more elegant or more contemporary. When I open the bathroom door to leave, there stands Keem. He grabs me and pulls me into the men's restroom, into a stall. He kisses me deep. It feels so good, but I pull away. What if someone comes in? I'm not worried about Menard; he just used the restroom, not to mention that I left my purse at the table. He would rather piss on himself than walk with my clutch in his hand.

"What are you doing, Rakeem?"

He hates when I call him by his government name.

"Why are you acting like this, She?"

"Acting like what?"

"Like you aren't fucking with me anymore."

"Because I'm not. That was your decision; now stand by that shit."

"I'm doing this to protect us, protect you."

"I'm a big girl. I can handle myself."

"I know you can, but I would never forgive myself if something happened to you."

"Well, I'm no longer your concern, now am I?"

I attempt to leave the stall. He puts his hand on the door to stop me from opening it and kisses me on the back of my neck. He uses his free hand to grope my breast.

"I love you, Sheree."

"Rakeem, stop it. I have to go."

Someone enters the restroom. The smell of cheap cologne overpowers my nose. It isn't Menard. Keem's hand is over my mouth.

"Shhhh!" he says.

His free hand runs down my body and under my skirt. He realizes I'm not wearing any panties and lets out a moan. I can feel his dick rising and pressing up against my back. He begins to rub my clit. I'm afraid to moan for fear of being heard. The man flushes the toilet and begins to wash his hands. I moan a little, sure he can't hear me over the water and the hand dryer. As he exits the bathroom, I orgasm and moan louder.

Keem removes his hand and is trying to unbuckle his belt. I fix my skirt and take a deep breath. I leave the stall and head to the women's restroom to freshen up. I hear Keem calling after me, but I ignore him. Thankfully, it is empty. I wet some paper towels and clean myself up the best I can. I return to my seat as Menard is paying the bill.

"You okay, babe? What took you so long?"

"That dessert must have had a lot of milk in it. It tore my stomach up. Let's get out of here before I have to use the restroom again."

"You aren't as young as you use to be. You know you're lactose intolerant." He laughs.

"Yeah; what was I thinking?" I respond.

We have to walk past Keem and Courtney to leave. I roll my eyes at him and mouth, "Fuck you." Nothing has changed in my eyes. I'm still not fucking with him. Not until I'm ready. But I'm appreciative of the orgasm.

I can always count on him to sexually take me to the next level, but I'm still pissed at him. It's going to take more than a little foreplay in a bathroom stall to get back in my good graces. It's time to check in with Lex to see what the next move is. Their last encounter didn't produce anything worth discussing. According to Lex, Courtney isn't interested sexually, but I know Lex. She isn't going to stop. Courtney letting her perform oral sex on her was the green light she needed. She is more determined than ever to turn Courtney out. There is a Chanel bag riding on it.

~ Twenty-Three ~

Rakeem

What are the odds of me running into Sheree and her punk-ass husband at the restaurant? So, now the nigga wants to man up and take his woman to an upscale restaurant? Wow! And the nerve of her to act as if she isn't missing a nigga! I know she does. I can tell by how wet her pussy was when I put my finger in it. I know she isn't getting wet like that for that nigga. Please! I know her ass better not still have me blocked. It has been over a week since the restaurant. She'd better be over her attitude. Let me text her ass.

Me: *Good afternoon sweetie!*

My phone beeps. I look at my phone pissed off. She still has me blocked! This ma'fucka has lost her mind! Yeah, I told her we had to chill, but that doesn't mean cut a nigga off completely! I am beyond pissed. Pacing the floor pissed. She's got me fucked up if she thinks she's going to play me like this. Fuck that! She must not remember I know where she works, where she lives. I should go over and blow her marriage straight up. Damn! I sound like a straight sucker! I told her we needed to chill, and I'm mad because she's chillin'! *LOL.*

Karma is a bitch! We men can't stand a taste of our own medicine. I can admit that. I haven't had sex with Courtney since the restaurant because my dick wants Sheree. Sure, I could get it up and bust one if I want to with Courtney, but that's what *he* wants.

'Wait a minute… I still have her direct number at work. I will call private. If she's available, I know she'll answer. I'll give her a call. But what will I say?'

I call my boy Rod. He always speaks the truth, even if I don't want to hear it.

"What up, doe?"

"What up, my nigga?"

"Shit, chilling at the crib before making my rounds to replenish these vending machines."

Rod is one of the few ambitious and successful friends I have. He started off with one vending machine. He now has over twenty vending machines in Detroit as well as the suburban areas. He is currently working on something big, but doesn't want to let the cat out the bag just yet.

"That's what's up. Man, per usual, your boy's got woman problems."

"Nigga! So, do I!"

"What?! Not you! Not the male gigolo. What problems could you possibly have?" I laugh.

"Man, how much time you got? We should meet at Truth. I could use a drink… or two."

"It's like that?"

"Yeah, man; it's like that."

"Okay. What time can you get up there?"

"I can be there in an hour."

"Same here."

Okay; see you soon."

"One."

"One."

Truth Gentlemen Club is located on East Eight Mile Road. It is one of several strip clubs that stretch from east to west on Eight Mile. There are four things you can find driving from one side of "The Mile" to the other: strip clubs, liquor stores, weed dispensaries, and pussy. Whoever thought about lining all that shit up together was a fucking genius because they all go hand-in-hand. After niggas get drunk (liquor store) and high (dispensary), they want to eat and see some ass shaking (strip club). After all that ass shaking, they get horny, so they want to fuck (strip club or the crackhead freaks selling ass on The Mile)! One stop shop!

Strip clubs are not how they use to be. Now women visit them more than men do. When I asked several females why, they say for the food. That may be somewhat true, but I'm sure they are also scouting out their next meal ticket. Hoes always tryna come up on their next big come up.

Rod and I arrive at Truth at the same time. His Camaro is blinging from the custom paint job. Depending on the angle, the car appears to be dark green or black. It is sitting on a pair of twenty-six-inch black Ruccis that make it stand out from the rest. It is a beast. Rod steps out matching his car. He is Gucci from head to toe. No big, noticeable-ass G's, but I know it's Gucci because of the signature red and green stripes on his collar. Same with his sneakers.

Me, I'm a label head as well, when I want to be. Today I've settled for something low-key. A simple hunter green Ralph Lauren Polo jogging suit with wheat Timberlands. Jogging suits are my go-to when I want to just get up and go. I splashed on a little Creed cologne for good measure. When I dress down, I wear an expensive cologne, and when I wear expensive, designer labels, I wear what I consider "every day" cologne, like Dolce & Gabbana, Polo, or Versace. Some call it weird, but I call it being me.

We give each other dap, pay the cover charge, and enter the club. It is midafternoon, so it is fairly empty except for a few suits-and-ties and local drug dealers conducting "business meetings". There are a few girls playing around on the pole. Some are practicing moves for a possible act, while others are dancing for the few occupants who are front and center of the stage. Rod and I opt for a booth near the back. I'm really not there to be entertained. I have enough women issues on my hands, and I'm sure Rod feels the same way. A petite, brown-skinned chick comes to take our drink orders. She has a small frame and weave down to her ass.

"What can I get you fellas?"

"Two shots of Patron and a Corona," I say.

"Bring me the same, with some limes as well."

"Got it. Would you fellas need a menu?"

"Yeah, that's cool," Rod says.

Ms. Petite walks away and I go right in on Rod. I want to hear what women problems he has. He usually doesn't let women get to him. When one acts up, he simply cuts her off and replaces her.

"Man, what kind of women problems do you have?"

"You know that chick Angie I was telling you about?"

"Yeah; the registered nurse down at Receiving Hospital."

"This bish is crazy!"

"What you mean, crazy?"

"Man, this hoe pulled up on me and April at Benihana's the other day."

"Wow!"

"She must have followed me to April's house, which meant she was waiting at my house."

"Get the fuck outta here!"

"She waited until we were seated around a group of ma'fuckas before she walked in and showed her natural black ass!"

I couldn't hold back my laughter.

"It ain't funny, my nigga!" he said, although he was laughing when he said it.

"She started telling April how she was just with me the night before, and that it was her pussy she was kissing when she kissed my lips."

"What did April say?"

"Nothing at first. Then she reached over and stuck her tongue down my throat, kissing the shit out of me. When she was done, she looked over at Angie and told her that her pussy tasted really good and she could join us after dinner tonight so she could taste her pussy firsthand."

By this time, I was laughing so hard I had tears coming out my eyes.

"Shiiid, nigga! That don't sound like it ended bad at all."

"That ain't the end. Angie was livid at April's response. She tried to reach over and snatch April out the chair. I almost fell out the chair trying to stop her from getting at April. Thank God Security came and escorted her off the premises. They threatened to call the cops if she didn't leave. Reality must have kicked in and she remembered she had a nursing license because she got the fuck on. But that didn't stop her from pulling up to my house last night. Stalking!"

"Oh yeah? What'd you do?"

"I called the police on her ass! I told them there was a strange car that had been sitting there for hours. Shit, you know they don't play out there. And she's black! They came, tapped on her window, said a few words, and she got the fuck on."

"Damn, man! You called the po-po on her?"

"Not on her, per se; on a suspicious car. I don't want her to lose her license, but if she keeps fucking with me, she's going to lose more than that."

Rod isn't for any games when it comes to domestic violence. He doesn't fuck with anyone and expects the same in return. His sister was murdered by her ex-husband ten years ago when she tried to leave him. He'd turned himself in and was sentenced to life without the possibility of parole. He never got the chance to serve out his sentence. On Rod's sister's birthday, five years ago, he was murdered in prison, beaten to death in the yard with a barbell. Prison guards didn't even notice him until the yard cleared. He lay on the utility bench lifeless, with a broken neck and a battered face. There was talk Rod had ordered the hit, but he'd never admitted it, not even to me.

"I hear you, man. These broads are crazy as fuck. Your life over theirs all day long. Hell, my problems seem minute as hell compared to the shit you've been going through."

"Perhaps. What you got going on?"

He summons the petite waitress to bring us another round of drinks and take our food order. He orders the surf-n-turf and I order blackened salmon, rice pilaf, and asparagus.

"Man, Court and I ran into Sheree and her husband at Ocean Prime about a week ago."

"Word?! What the hell happened?"

"She tried to ghost me. I texted her when her husband went to the restroom and she blocked me. Right there! Blocked me!"

"Hell nah!" He laughed.

"Yeah, but I followed her ass right into the restroom."

"You did what? Nigga, how did you know Courtney wasn't going to walk in?"

"Because she had just gone to the restroom. Besides, I snatched her as she was coming out and pulled her into the men's restroom."

"Well, how did you know her husband wasn't going to come in?"

"Because he had just used the restroom also. Anyway, I took her in the stall and played with her pussy until she came. I tried to get some of that, but she busted out the stall, told me not to contact her, and left!"

"Damn, that was a boss move."

"I know, nigga, because I'm a boss," I say as I pop my collar.

"Nigga, I'm talking about her!" He laughs. "She got her rocks off and gave your ass the deuces sign." He laughs again, throwing up deuces.

"Shut the hell up, dog! Then, as she was leaving, she mouthed, 'Fuck You,' and rolled her eyes. I haven't heard from her since!"

"Nigga, your feelings and pride are hurt!" He laughed.

"Whatever, nigga. She ain't got to be like that. I was tryna protect her from Courtney."

"Nah, you got scared you were about to be caught up. You got spooked and ended it, but you really didn't want to."

"Yeah, you're right, but she ain't got to take it that far. She's the one who's married. I should be treating her like this, not the other way around."

"You're right, but you gave her ass the upper hand. She has the juice; now you have to somehow gain back control."

"Yeah, I do."

"What're you gonna do?"

"I don't know."

"Let me ask you a serious question."

"Shoot," I say as I down a shot and chase it with the lime.

"Do you really think she would leave her husband for you? Would you want and be able to trust her if she did? And do you really love Courtney enough to marry her?"

"I don't know, man."

"To which question?"

"All three of them."

"Damn, man. You've got it bad."

"I know."

"You do know you're in love with a married woman, right?"

"Yeah, I do."

"And you do know you aren't in love with Courtney, right? You're just tolerating and using her because you don't want to be alone."

"Yeah, I know."

"And you know eventually you're going to have to address and seek the answer to all three questions, right?"

"Yep."

"My nigga, my shit may be fucked up, but your shit is way deeper."

"Tell me about it." I take a swig of my Corona.

"Man, let's get a dance from these broads and get out of here."

"I'm with you."

He summons two dancers to our booth. I can't enjoy the dance because so many thoughts are dancing in my head. I have so much to think about. I am no longer in the mood to talk to Sheree. I just want to be alone in my thoughts. I have some decisions to make.

~ Twenty-Four ~

Courtney

Things haven't been the same for the last few weeks. Rakeem seems to be more distant than usual. Not sure what has happened, but it seemed to start after we had dinner at Ocean Prime. It was one of our favorite restaurants that seemed to never disappoint. That night wasn't any different. I got my usual: scallops, shrimp, asparagus, and jasmine rice. My drink of choice was Berries & Bubbles. It is a nice combination of brown liqueur, white vodka, wine, and juices over dry smoke. After a few of those, I was ready for anything.

My phone was vibrating like crazy in my purse. I pulled it out to see Alexis had called and texted me several times. Rakeem's mind seemed to be somewhere else; I wasn't sure he even noticed. I excused myself to use the restroom. After using it, I called Alexis back to see what was so important. We hadn't spoken much since our last dinner date when she'd returned my shirt and vice versa.

Me:	*Hello?*
Alexis:	*Hey! How are you doing?*
Me:	*I'm fine. What's the matter? Something wrong?*
Alexis:	*No! Nothing wrong. Just wanted to see you.*
Me:	*You're back in town?*

Alexis:	*Yes. Just tryna tie up a few ends. How about dinner tomorrow?*
Me:	*I'll see what I can do.*
Alexis:	*Okay. See you tomorrow.*
Me:	*SMH... no promises.*
Alexis:	*Send me a picture.*
Me:	*No... TTYL*
Alexis:	*Damn, it's like that?*

I headed out the restroom without responding. Rakeem was fumbling with his phone. He looked up when I returned to the table and spoke.

"You good?"

"Yes, I am. What about you? You seemed to be a little distracted."

"Yeah, I'm good. Work ish."

Rakeem was a street nigga turned business owner. He had turned his drug money into a legit business. He had several car washes, barbershops, and beauty salons across the City of Detroit. He held meetings with managers once a week at a different offsite location, usually a restaurant or strip club. He wasn't keen with keeping the same routine; so much betrayal and disloyalty in the drug game had taught him better. Collecting money, checking on day-to-day operations, getting caught up, and discussing future endeavors were his main focal points during these meetings. He liked being behind the scenes of his operations. The less he was seen or heard meant the less people could pinpoint his moves. Or the fewer people who would be able to point him out in a lineup, depending on the situation.

After Rakeem shut me down about discussing the wedding, I was kind of annoyed. I felt my phone vibrate again. Since Rakeem was on his phone, I pulled mine out as well. It was another text from Lex. I opened the attachment and saw a picture of Alexis in a red one-piece teddy. Her body was stunning. No filters needed. Her waist is small, and her breasts are nice and perky. The caption read: *Hope to see you tomorrow for dinner.*

I responded with a simple happy face emoji.

I ordered another drink as Rakeem went to the restroom. I scrolled on Facebook and Instagram for a minute, took a selfie of myself, and made a post with caption reading: *Good living and good food with my babe.* I sent Alexis the same selfie. I knew I was egging her on, but I was bored and feeling unwanted. Alexis was giving me all the attention and accolades I wanted from Rakeem. There was no chance I would ever think of being in a long-term relationship with a woman. Short-term either. Sure, I'd let her eat the box; I had been intoxicated. That's my story and I'm sticking to it. I'd had no intention of seeing Alexis again. She lived out of town. According to her, she and her boyfriend were on the outs, so I wasn't sure what other business she had in Detroit.

Alexis and I texted back and forth until Rakeem returned to the table. He seemed to be in better spirits.

He took a long drag from his beer and continued to eat in silence. I decided to make small talk.

"What plans do you have for the weekend?"

"Nothing much—work, chilling, hanging."

"What about chilling or hanging with me?"

"Courtney, my life doesn't revolve around you. Let's just enjoy the night."

"You act like you can't stand me lately. What's going on with you? Are you still mad because I came in late?"

"I'm so past that. It ain't that serious."

"Something is."

"Look! Stop—"

He stopped talking as a couple walked past our table, most likely on their way out the door. He made brief eye contact before taking a deep breath and continuing to speak.

"Stop nagging me. This weekend, I plan on doing what I want to do. If that consists of you, I'll let you know. More than likely, I'll be doing me. I expect you to do the same."

I nodded my head in defeat, took out my phone, and texted Lex.

Me: *What time is dinner?*

Alexis: *Seven* 😊

Me: Ok. Text me when you confirm a location.

Alexis: Will do.

I swear Rakeem was getting on my last nerve, with his nonchalant ass.

Sometimes I wonder if he is acting like this to deter me from marrying him. This is the closest I've come to marrying someone, and I refuse to give it all up. My parents and I have been waiting all my life for me to walk down the aisle. Unless another man magically appears to take my hand in marriage, Rakeem is going to be my husband. Sure, I've entertained Lex' advances, but I have no plans of dealing with her in that manner. She is around for a good time, not a long time. Rakeem isn't giving me the attention I want or need. I wonder if he is still dealing with the mystery woman. He has been home a lot lately. The few times I followed him, he was where he said he was going. There aren't any signs he is out creeping, although he clearly suspected I was the night I came home late.

We skipped dessert and headed home. The ride home was silent. He hummed to some rap song on the radio while I looked out the window and daydreamed. I wondered how my life would be if I'd decided to have kids and lived my life according to my parents' plan versus my plan.

My parents are devoted Christians. Bible study every Wednesday. Choir rehearsal on Fridays, and church, morning and afternoon service, every Sunday. I was told how to dress, where to go, and what to do until I was twenty-one years old. When I tried to stand up to my parents, they would antagonize or manipulate me until I did it their way. They had a way of making me do what they wanted me to do without directly saying anything by using the Bible as a weapon. Whenever I did something they didn't approve, they whipped out the Bible and slapped the shit out me with a Scripture.

When I got pregnant at twenty-one, my mother had harassed me until I'd gotten an abortion. She'd told me God would never forgive me if I had a baby out of wedlock. After having the abortion, I'd gone to my gynecologist and gotten on long-term birth control. From the age of twenty-one, I had several IUD's until I decided to get my tubes tied. I don't want to bring a baby into the world and inflict the same shit on a child that my mother and father inflicted on me. But the main reason I don't want to have a baby is because I don't want to give them the satisfaction of having grandchildren. I'm an only child. The only thing they want in the world, outside of me getting married, is for me to make them grandparents.

Am I punishing myself in the process? Maybe, but truthfully, I've never felt I was the motherly type. I barely like kids. Hell, Rakeem's kids are enough. I can't wait for them to go home when they come over. They are so needy and require all of his attention. It has gotten to the point that I make up excuses to exclude myself. He tries to persuade me to join them in a movie or a game, but I decline and tell him that his bond with them is more important and I don't want to intrude.

The garage door opening pulls me out of my trance. Rakeem punches in the code to disarm the alarm system.

He immediately begins to peel off his clothes and heads for the shower. Any other time, I would've loved to join him, but his coldness toward me is weighing me down. I have no desire to be in his presence.

I go to the kitchen and pour me a glass of champagne. I grab the bottle of melatonin, open it, and retrieve two. I place them in my mouth and chase them with the glass of bubbly deliciousness, then pour another glass. I walk to the window and stare outside. It is so calm, peaceful, undisturbed—all the things lacking in my life. I feel so empty on the inside, unhappy, unfulfilled. A single tear rolls down my left cheek.

I am so tired of faking it, but this is all I know to do. Being the real Courtney would disappoint so many people. It is fucking up my mental; I feel it. Staying sane is getting harder and harder. I feel like a pressure cooker about to explode. Tomorrow, I will call in my prescription. I can't afford to fall apart right now. I'm almost at the finish line.

I down the rest of my champagne and proceed to the bedroom. I remove my clothes and climb under the covers. Seeing Lex tomorrow is a necessity. I need someone to make me feel wanted and loved. I need to be around someone who doesn't judge me, someone I can be myself around. I need sanity.

ଔ✺ଞ

I wake up the next morning to the smell of bacon and pancakes. Rakeem is in a decent mood. He doesn't see or hear me enter because his back is toward me.

"Good morning."

"Morning. I made breakfast. Yours is in the microwave if you want it."

"Thanks."

He is already dressed. The kitchen is almost clean as well. My guess is he tried to leave before I awoke. I ask if he is about to leave.

"Yes; I have a lot of business to handle today. Business is going well on all fronts, and I must keep it that way."

"Yeah, well, at least something is getting some attention around here," I mumble.

He turns around to face me, smirking. "I'm going to act as if that wasn't directed at me. I give my attention to the things or people I think deserve it. When something feels off, I don't try to force it."

"What are you trying to say?"

"I'm saying this—us—feels forced. You can't tell me you don't feel it too."

"Yes, I do feel like something is a little off, but I'm hoping we can work it out and come back together as one."

He doesn't say anything, so I continue.

"Maybe we need to go to counseling or something. I love you, Rakeem. I don't want this to end without fighting for it."

"Some things are not worth fighting for."

"Is that some things *our relationship*?" I'm getting heated.

"I don't know, Courtney." He exhales. "I guess we'll see."

"I will set up a counseling session." I wrap my arms around his waist and lay my head on his chest. "You are the best thing in my life. I don't want it to end without giving it all we got."

"I hear you. Set it up. It can't make it any worse."

He hugs me back. This is the first bit of affection he has shown in a couple of weeks. It feels good, but it still isn't enough. It isn't enough to fill me up to keep me going. I am low on fuel. I need Alexis to make me feel full again. I need her to replenish me so I can keep pushing forward. I am suffocating without it. I need her to keep me alive. Literally. The lack of attention Rakeem is showing me is killing me.

~ Twenty-Five ~

Alexis

To say I am ecstatic Courtney has agreed to have dinner with me is an understatement. I am in another funk because Peyton is acting like an ass. We stay on the outs because he isn't ready to give me the relationship I deserve. I'm tired of being kept behind closed doors. I know I'm supposed to be just fucking with Courtney to sabotage her relationship with Rakeem, but the truth of the matter is, I kind of like her.

I would never tell Sheree this because I'm loyal to her. I will never betray our friendship for no outside-ass bitch. She held it down and looked out for me when no one else would. See, I have never quite fit in with the white or the black kids because I am biracial—black mother, Mexican father. I was teased about everything in school, from the way I dressed to the way I talked. The only thing I had going for me was my curly black hair and tinted brown skin. But that wasn't enough to keep the mean-ass kids from taunting me every chance they got.

It wasn't until I met Sheree in middle school that my life started to change for the better. With money she earned babysitting, we would ride the bus across town to the thrift store. She would buy me an outfit per week. Usually, I bought an additional shirt so it appeared I had two outfits, when, really, I would just change out the shirt. She taught me that as well. She also taught me to hold my head high and to start to love myself from within. It took all of middle school for me to do that.

By the time we reached high school, I was a changed person. I was confident in the skin I was in and my popularity went through the roof. I was still shopping out of thrift stores, but no one could tell. The way I threw shit together had everybody wanting to be dressed by yours truly. I got so cool with the employees that I started working there part-time. I got first dibs on the designer items before they hit the floor. I started hitting all the thrift stores in the suburban areas. I would purchase the items and resell them at a higher cost to my classmates. I was voted best dressed of the senior class! I have Sheree to thank for all of that. She saved me in so many ways. She made "Alexis" the woman she is today. A real life, rags-to-riches story, chile!

I like Courtney because she is easy to talk to. It has been a long time since I've this way about a woman. She is sexy, smart, and a little bit devious; it is kind of intriguing. She makes me feel wanted because she is so needy. She can do so much better than Rakeem; he ain't shit. He and Sheree will never be over. As long as there is breath in both of their bodies, they will forever and always be like magnets. The kind of love they have is beautiful, but can be deadly as well. I have told Sheree to just get over him, but she swears she can't. How can you rationalize with a married woman who's in love with another man? You can't!

Today is the day I'll go all out on Courtney. I'll call her up to the hotel, and when she enters, she will automatically think the decorated room is set up for her. I will inform her it's for my 'boyfriend'. However, he will give me a call informing me he isn't able to make it. Now, I'm the distraught girlfriend who needs Courtney to lean on and to comfort me. Who can turn down a damsel in distress? Certainly not another distressed damsel! By the end of the night, I plan on having Courtney like Burger King—my way! I have a bag of tricks under the bed as well as in my purse to make the night go smoother.

    Courtney is set to arrive shortly. My phone begins to ring and I know it is Sheree. She's calling to make sure things are going according to plan. I make the mistake of informing her that I like Courtney and I'm having mixed feelings. She isn't buying that shit. She tells me to put on my big-girl panties and get the job done before hanging up on me. My phone beeps. It is an attachment from Sheree: the picture of the Chanel bag I want. No turning back now. I can feel the leather of the bag in my hands. The shit you do for friends—and a fucking label!

    I shower, lotion, and spray my body with one of my sweet-smelling flavored scents from Bath & Body Works. I turn on some smooth R & B and set the scene. I need to make sure everything is strategically placed and setup. Sheree, my *boyfriend*, is set to call me to cancel our date. I'm nervous as well as horny. I grab my purse and remove the small bottle with a tiny spoon inside. I scoop up the powdery substance on the spoon and sniff it up my nostrils. I need something to get the edge off. Some people's choice of drugs is weed, heroin, or crack. Mine is a little cocaine every now and again. I'm a recreational user.

    Courtney knocks on the hotel door. I am dressed in a cute two-piece skirt set with booties that show off my toned calves. She is equally cute in form-fitting jeans and a cute hot-pink, cropped top, fuzzy sweater. She has on a cute Gucci belt with the matching purse and boots. I am such a whore for labels that I'm getting turned on. I greet her with a hug and a kiss on the lips, but she turns away slightly, avoiding the kiss.

"You look scrumptious," I say.

"You look great as well, and you smell… delicious!"

"Hopefully, delicious enough to taste."

She laughs and shakes her head. She turns around and notices the room is laid out with unlit candles and rose pedals. In the middle of the floor is a table set for two and a bottle chilled with two champagne glasses and chocolate-covered strawberries. Food is to be ordered later, but the setup is all there. She places her hand over her mouth and gasps.

"Oh my God, Alexis! You shouldn't have done this! This is so sweet! I don't know what to say!"

I feel like shit for a minute, but I can't deter from the plan.

"Huh? Girl, this isn't for you! My boyfriend will be here shortly. I want to surprise him with a nice dinner! I figured you and I could go out for drinks. Food for you, an appetizer for me. Then I'll order something to go and serve it to my man like I cooked it! Brilliant, huh?"

"Wow! Yeah… Brilliant."

I hear the disappointment in her voice.

"Aww, Courtney! I'm so sorry. That sounded so harsh. I didn't mean to offend you."

"What? Girl, don't worry about it. It looks beautiful. I wish someone loved me the way you love your man. I can't even get my man to spend time with me. He's lucky to have you."

"Thanks, boo. Tell you what: I'll hook up with you next week." I walk closer to her. "I never want to see that look of disappointment on your face again. I never want to be the cause of that." I kiss her on her lips. This time she doesn't look away. She invites me in. I hug her tightly. She breaks the embrace and wipes her watery eyes.

"Okay, let's go get drinks."

Damn, she is emotional. This may be easier than expected.

The hotel is very upscale and includes a restaurant to match. We sit near the fireplace, sip drinks, and eat food over the crackle of the fire and the angelic sound of the harpist caressing the strings of the harp. We are both buzzing pretty good, touching and feeding each other. It feels so good to have someone genuinely interested in you—or the person she thinks you are. I order takeout for my *boyfriend*, and we head back upstairs. Courtney wants to head out, but I insist she stay and keep me company until he arrives. I have ordered a variety of food: shrimp, blackened salmon, lobster tails, baked potatoes, yellow rice, and a vegetable medley. Courtney helps me make the plates, light the candles, and pour more wine. We stand back and observe our work.

"PERFECT!" I yell, picking Courtney up and spinning her around. I give her a long kiss as she slides down my breasts. This time I break the embrace and we look in each other's eyes.

"I've got something I need to tell you," I tell Courtney. I am buzzing and starting to talk too much.

"What is it?"

"I—"

My phone rings. It is my *boyfriend*. I jump back into character.

"Hey, babe! Are you on your way? In the lobby?" I'm pretending to be super-excited.

"What do you mean, you can't make it? Why the hell not?!"

Silence.

"Do you have any idea what I planned for us? I'm looking at a bunch of food, champagne, and strawberries that are about to go to waste."

Silence.

"Yeah, you're sorry all right! A sorry piece of shit! I don't deserve this shit! I know I can find a man who loves me! I will not be your option two anymore! Lose my fucking number!"

I throw the phone against the wall, causing it to break, run to the bathroom, and continue with the performance of my life. Courtney knocks on the door, offering a lot of kind words. She asks me to come out and talk about it. I refuse the first three times. When I finally open the door,

Courtney is standing there with tears running down her cheeks.

"He doesn't deserve you, like Rakeem doesn't deserve me. We will get through this… together."

This time she kisses me. After what seems like forever, I break the kiss.

"Well, first things first. Help me eat some of this food." I lift the champagne glass and make a toast. "To new beginnings. Cheers!"

"Cheers!"

~ Twenty-Six ~

Courtney

I jump up in a panic and hurriedly lie back down. Not because I want to, but because the pain in my head forces me to. I have the most excruciating headache I have ever had. It feels as if I was hit by a Mack truck! Between my legs and ass are sore. I can't have been raped. I vaguely remember things getting rough, but have no actual recollection of what took place. I try to gather my thoughts and recall last night events. However, the last thing I recall is Alexis and me getting ready for the food and drinks in the hotel room. I call out her name.

"ALEXIS!" I yell, and instantly regret it.

I close my eyes and hold my hand up to my head as if that will calm down the trombone playing inside it. I open my eyes and look around the room. There's no sign Alexis is there. All her belongings are gone as well as the food tray I remember was setup in the middle of the floor. The rose pedals and candles that once draped the floor and beamed on the nightstand and jacuzzi are also gone. There is no trace of Alexis. Then I notice a small, handmade envelope with my name on it. I open it up and read it.

Dear Courtney,

I'm so sorry. I hope one day you can somehow forgive me. Thank you for appreciating the real me. Maybe I will see you in the next lifetime. Goodbye.

With Love,
Alexis

Now I am thoroughly confused. *'What the fuck is she sorry for? What is the real her? What is she talking about, goodbye? How long has she been gone?'*

According to my phone, it is 4 a.m. I know Rakeem will have a lot to say when he wakes up and I'm not there, but I really don't care. If he was spending time with me, I wouldn't have to spend my time elsewhere. He also mentioned that this relationship feels forced, so he doesn't really see us in a relationship at all. Despite everything I'm thinking, I still want to be with him and make things work. I'll just tell him the ladies and I went to the strip club following the bar. I know it's farfetched, but it isn't like it couldn't happen.

I gather my belongings to leave, still confused and unable to recall what happened last night. I need some more sleep. That may be the problem.

On the way home, I stopped at the gas station and grabbed a Stanback and a Vernors, not giving a fuck about any danger that could be lurking. I open the powdery substance, lift my tongue, and pour it in my mouth. With my head tilted, I open the Vernors and drink until it's halfway gone. I'm hoping to no longer taste the remnants of the potent medicine.

As I drive home, I'm thinking about the lie I'm going to tell Rakeem. This is so out of my character. At one point in time, I never would have stepped out on him—let alone with a female! His actions are part of the reason I have done so, but that is no excuse. I should be woman enough to leave if he is unwilling or unable to treat me the way I deserve to be treated. *So, why am I not leaving?* I know why. I don't want to be alone. I don't want to start over at fifty. I have found a man who, at one time, thought he wanted to be with me for the rest of his life. Now he isn't sure. I can hear my mother's voice in my head.

"Stick with this one, Courtney. Your biological clock is ticking away and you aren't getting any younger. Having a piece of man at your age is better than having no man at all."

The pressure my parents put on me, especially my mother, is smothering. She makes me feel I am less than a woman because I am unmarried and childless. She often goes on to say that having children and being married ratifies my place as a woman. I don't believe it wholeheartedly, but she obviously does.

I take a deep breath as I pull into the driveway. I know Rakeem is sleep, so I have time to catch some Z's as well before having to explain myself. I remove my clothes and put them down the laundry chute. I carefully kick off my shoes so I don't wake Rakeem. When I go to our bedroom, he isn't there. I peep in the guestroom where he appears to be sleeping. It is hard to tell because his head is turned the opposite way. However, something feels off. I can't put my finger on it. It isn't uncommon for one of us to sleep in the guest bedroom when we are mad at each other, but there is something else that feels alarming. Unable to function properly due to my lingering headache, I decide to call it a night and address it tomorrow. I go back to our bedroom and collapse on the bed. I think I'm sleep before my head hits the pillow.

꿈✻꿈

I'm awakened by the television blaring loudly in the other room. I can't make out what is being said, but I can tell it is women talking, laughing, singing, and giggling. I put my pillow over my head and try to go back to sleep. My headache has subsided, but my mind is still foggy and I feel immensely fatigued. Despite my desperate attempts to block out the noise from the TV, I can't. I want to tell him to turn it down, but I don't want to wake a sleeping bear. I'm not sure if he knows what time I came in or not.

After about five minutes of low chitter-chatter, I conclude he has reduced the volume... until I hear what sounds like moaning.

'Did he switch the channel to porn?'

I look at my phone and see it is noon. I text Alexis good morning and wait for her response. My message comes back undeliverable. I think, *'That's weird,'* and send it again. I get the same response. I sit up in the bed and call her phone number. The automated message says, "This number is no longer in service." I try several more times to make sure. I even look at my phone to make sure I'm calling the right number.

'What the fuck is going on?!'

I am getting more and more pissed off. Alexis disappeared on me and Rakeem's watching porn in the middle of the day—I have had it! The moaning is louder, followed by ass-smacking and what sounds like a man asking the woman to say his name. She screams out "ALEXIS!" Her voice sounds like mine, but higher pitched. I creep to the door slowly, my heart beating a mile a minute, my breathing very shallow. I open the door and step slowly and softly into the living room. I don't want Rakeem aware of my appearance just yet. I have to get closer to make sure my ears aren't deceiving me.

Alexis is pounding me from the back. She has a handful of my hair as she's kissing me in my mouth. I am bouncing on her as if she has a dick! I can't believe I allowed her to use a strap-on to fuck me! I seem to be enjoying it like it was the real thing! I stand frozen, unable to move, with my mouth wide open. She removes her dick from my pussy and turns me around to face her as she shifts, slowing, obviously for the camera. I kiss her breast for a moment before she pushes my head downward to her dick! I gasp so loud that Rakeem turns around.

"You're awake! Come, sit down and enjoy the show. This is some real freaky shit!" He laughs.

I barely hear a word he says because I am too focused on Alexis mouth-fucking me! A deep baritone voice brings me out my trance.

"Yeeeaaah! Suck my dick, Courtney! Your mouth feels so good."

I watch myself enjoy sucking Alexis' dick before she removes it and instructs me bend over. I feel tears flow down my face and my legs start to get weak. However, I can't stop watching! I watch Alexis tongue-kiss my asshole as she is fingering my pussy. Then she reverses it and fingers my asshole as she kisses and licks my pussy. I must have really enjoyed it because I'm making noises I've never made before. After removing several fingers from my ass, she spits in it as she strokes herself.

She looks slightly in the direction of the camera, but still careful not to expose herself entirely. That's when I notice the chiseled, manly features of her face. Never once did I notice them before! I focus back on her stroking herself. Beads of sweat mixed with tears flow down my face. I feel like I'm having a panic attack and hyperventilating at the same time. Rakeem looks back at me, smirks, and offers me a seat.

"Come, sit down. You don't look so good."

He directs his attention back to the camera just as I scream in what seems to be pleasure and pain. Alexis has just forced her dick into my ass! I feel my legs give out and hear a loud thump as I hit the floor. I hear Rakeem's footsteps running toward me and him calling my name before everything goes black. My life flashes before my eyes as I lie there, unable to respond to Rakeem.

'Is this the end for me? I never got a chance to get married. Never got the chance to tell my parents I love them. Never got a chance to live my life the way I wanted. So many regrets.'

I feel more tears run down my cheek. That is the last thing I feel before complete darkness sets in and I am unable to feel anymore. I am dying, unmarried and unfulfilled. It is over.

To be continued…..

~ Questions ~

1. Do you think Sheree's plot to get Courtney out the picture was justified?
2. Alexis/Lex was in a difficult position. Have you ever been so loyal to a friend that you compromised your integrity? Or did something unethical?
3. Do you think Sheree and Rakeem's relationship was based on love or lust?
4. Who was the most selfish character in the book?
5. Which character (if any) could you relate to the most? Why?
6. What have you sacrificed for family (career, love, happiness, etc.)? Any regrets?
7. Do you think Sheree would ever leave Menard to be with Rakeem? If so, would they be able to fully trust each other?
8. What do you think Rakeem was thinking as he played the video of Courtney and Alexis (e.g., hurt, emotionless, relieved, etc.)?
9. What do you think Alexis/Lex was most sorry for?
10. Do you believe someone can be in love with two people at the same time?

Coming Soon...

The Dom
by Crystal Kinn-Tarver

Prologue

I arrived home later than usual. It was a crazy day at the eastside location. Money coming up short, customers not wanting to pay, and constant bickering amongst the women of the house. It is true what they say: Too many women in one household is never a good thing. They can't get along for shit! I had to threaten to fire or relocate their asses to a different location if they didn't get along. Usually, I didn't involve myself in the civil matters of the household, but I was between managers. Finding a replacement was harder than I'd thought it would be.

Before getting out the car, I removed my keys from my purse and surveyed the area. It was a habit I had established as a teenager. Always check your surroundings. A lot of shit lurks in the dark. Tonight was one of those nights.

Unlocking the door, I saw a shadow out the side of my eye. Before I had a chance to get a good look, it charged at me, forcing me inside the house. The force knocked us both to the floor, spilling most of the contents of my purse. My keys flew in one direction and my cellphone in another. The assailant regained his composure first and started toward me. I tried to stand, but my ankle was throbbing, preventing me from putting pressure on it.

Although his face was covered with a mask, his body build was quite familiar. Frozen in thought, trying to connect the dots, proved to be detrimental because he pounced on me. He fumbled with my pants as I tried to fight him off. He was much stronger than I was. I screamed for help, but he quickly muffled my mouth with his massive hands. He spoke for the first time.

"You stupid bitch! All you had to do was what I asked of you! But you wanted to have morals!"

Judge Barelli! *Unable to speak, my eyes widened. He noticed he had fucked up because I recognized his voice. The judge wanted a service I had refused to provide. Even in this grimy, cutthroat business, there were still some rules you shouldn't break. No exceptions! The judge didn't want to hear that shit. He wanted what he wanted. He had taken advantage of every service I had to offer and was one of my best customers. But he was spoiled, addicted, powerful—a deadly combination when provoked. With nothing more to hide, he removed his mask.*

"Yes, it's me! Why didn't you just give me what I wanted, Mi Amor? Instead, you tried to blackmail me! Despite what you think, I would never expose you. Never! But you?! You have the power to destroy my livelihood! Everything I've work for could be gone! I can't have that."

I continued to listen to him rant as sweat poured from his face, mixing with my tears.

"Since you didn't give me my initial fantasy, I guess I'll have to settle for my second fantasy—you!"

Reality started to set in. This motherfucker was going to rape and kill me!

I bit down on his hand hard enough for him to let me go. I kicked him in his balls and he rolled onto his back. I spotted my purse and hurriedly crawled toward it. He grabbed my bad leg and I screamed from the pain. I used my other leg to kick him in the face. Blood spilled from his nose onto my dark hardwood floors. I scrambled through my purse and found what I was looking for—my gun. I removed it from my purse and cocked it. He took notice and scurried toward the door, but not before I let off three shots.

Boom! Boom! Boom!

Gun in hand, I looked for my cellphone and spotted it on the opposite side of the room. I crawled toward it, careful not to take my eye off the door. I called 9-1-1.

"9-1-1. What is your emergency?"

"I would like to report an intruder!" I whispered, unsure of the judge whereabouts.

"Is the perpetrator still on the premises?"

"I'm not sure. He ran out the door. I shot him! Well, at least I think I did."

"So, there are weapons inside the home?"

"Yes! I'm licensed to carry."

"Okay, ma'am. Did you get a good look at his face?"

What should I say! If I say yes and he survived, he could take down my whole organization just to save his ass.

"Ma'am! Are you still there? Hello?"

"Yes, I'm still here! No. No, I didn't get a good look at him. He had on a mask."

"Okay. We have the address in the system. A car and ambulance are on the way."

"Thank you."

"You're welcome. Please stay on the line until they arrive."

"Okay."

As I stayed on the line, I got the courage to limp to the door. I didn't hear anything, so I knew the judge was either on my porch dead or he had gotten away. I looked out the door and the judge was nowhere in sight, but his blood was. He had been hit. Now that I knew I hadn't killed him, it was time to put another plan in motion.

It was too bad he hadn't killed me because I was going to make sure he suffered immensely. His livelihood was going to be the least of his worries. Now, I wanted his dignity, his money, AND his life. Nothing short of a miracle was going to stop me from taking all three. Nothing…

೧೩✸೨೦

Made in the USA
Columbia, SC
09 June 2022